"I let her die, Matt.

God forgive me, because I know I never can forgive myself. I swear to you that I didn't know I was leaving her to die. I would have died a thousand times in her place."

Before Matt could speak, a disk of green glowing light suddenly appeared on his father's forehead. The light shifted across his father's face, elongating and pinching as it tracked the craggy features.

Fear blazed through Matt's heart. He turned, knotted his fist in his father's shirtfront, then saw the green glowing light flit down over one of Lord Brockton's eyes.

Before Matt could pull his father away from the light, something sizzled in the air between them. In that instant, his father's eye disappeared, leaving a blackened hole the size of Matt's thumb.

Slowly Lord Brockton fell forward. In a nightmarish moment, Matt saw the flames in the fireplace through his father's head.

There was no blood, only a clean, empty hole and the smell of burnt flesh.

"Father!" Matt yelled even though he knew he couldn't have survived such a wound. And then he noticed the green glowing light had settled over his own h

Don't miss the next

HUNTER'S LEAGUE

The Mystery Unravels

HUNTER'S LEAGUE

A CONSPIRACY REVEALED

MEL ODOM

SIMON PULSE
New York London Toronto Sydney

For Dan Hanttula, Dave Kirby, Shiloh Odom, and Sterling Gates. We're the million-dollar Wednesday night NTN hopefuls, guys.

This book is a work of fiction. Any references to historical events, real people, or real locales are used fictitiously. Other names, characters, places, and incidents are the product of the author's imagination, and any resemblance to actual events or locales or persons, living or dead, is entirely coincidental.

SIMON PULSE
An imprint of Simon & Schuster Children's Publishing Division
1230 Avenue of the Americas, New York, NY 10020
Copyright © 2005 by Mel Odom
All rights reserved, including the right of reproduction in whole or in part in any form.
SIMON PULSE and colophon are registered trademarks of Simon & Schuster, Inc.
Designed by Sammy Yuen Jr.
The text of this book was set in Palatino.
Manufactured in the United States of America
First Simon Pulse edition January 2005
10 9 8 7 6 5 4 3 2 1

Library of Congress Control Number 2004107831
ISBN 0-689-86608-9

Chapter 1

Matt Hunter stared at his father seated beside him in the jarring, narrow confines of the hansom cab bouncing through the potholes in the twisting street.

The feverish look on his father's face had blanched his lean features, aided by the occasional gaslight lamp on the streets. Perspiration tracked the elder Hunter's cheeks in spite of the cool fall air that blew through the carriage's windows from the Thames River.

Like Matt, he wore a tight-fitting frock jacket with tails and a tall silk hat. Matt held his own hat in his hands between his knees. He knew an observer would immediately recognize them as father and son. At seventeen years old, he was slightly taller than his father, almost six feet, but built broad-shouldered and lean like Roger Hunter. Matt's black hair came from his father, but his emerald green eyes were from his mother.

Is this another wild-goose chase? Matt wondered. *Another insane safari that will brand my father a lunatic?*

Stories still circulated about the possibility his father had murdered his mother, but never once in the past seven years had Matt believed that it might be true. His father had loved his mother—and still loved her. Losing her had driven his father mad with guilt.

They were near the dockyards. The moon reflected from the Thames in the few places the low-lying dirty fog didn't blanket. Despite the sewer systems that had been put in under the metropolis during the last few years, the stench was atrocious. Matt recognized London Dock ahead on the left and St. Katherine's Dock on the right. The fogbound river lay straight ahead.

"Why are we here?" Matt asked.

His father gestured at the river. "Why, to look for a ship, of course."

"What ship?"

"You'll see, my boy. You'll see. A little patience is required. Just a little more." Roger Hunter—also known by his ancestral title of Lord Brockton, which had been granted to a forebear in the Hundred Years' War—swiveled his feverish gaze on his son, his hands knotting and unknotting on the head of his walking stick. "Once you know I'm not mad, as I know you've heard so many people say, you'll know that you have a proper father, my boy. I've been waging an undisclosed war against evil, against those who have relentlessly murdered in their efforts to topple the crown, may God save the Queen, and seize control of this country."

The rolling sickness returned to Matt's stomach. *He's deep into the madness now. There will be no pulling him out of his delusions tonight.*

Matt cursed the sense of guilt that had once more drawn him into his father's sphere of influence. During the seven years since her murder, it had become apparent that Angeline Hunter had been the glue that bound the two men in her life.

Matt had spent much of those seven years—including birthdays and holidays—alone. Or in the company of Herbert Finsterwald, his father's friend and majordomo at their ancestral estate.

But over the past year, Matt had often escaped that enforced solitude, and even kept a flat of his own in the city under a false name. He'd spent long nights in London, in the company of Paul Chadwick-Standish, a friend since childhood, or with Gabriel, a young thief who lived off whatever the dark, dangerous streets brought him.

Matt hadn't a clue what to do with his life, but he sometimes considered traveling with one of his father's ships just to get away from London and his father's madness. Doing that proved impossible, though. He could stay away from his father, but he couldn't desert him. As a result,

Matt's own life had been frozen, waiting to see what his father would do.

So when his father had come round earlier that evening to the modest flat Matt maintained—and how had he found out where it was? Matt wondered—the young man had felt he had no choice but to accompany the elder Hunter. He supposed it was guilt that made him see his father from time to time.

"Just stay with me, my boy," Lord Brockton said. "Stay with me and you'll see your old father has not gone soft in his head as so many believe."

The hansom cab bounced to a stop, and even before it settled Lord Brockton was out the door. His frock jacket snapped and popped in the wind.

Sweeping the river with his gaze and spotting all the ships at anchor, Matt didn't know how his father hoped to find one ship among so many. He caught the stink of coal stored on barges, fish from the fishing boats, and the hearty aroma of coffee beans and tobacco from cargo vessels that had traveled from the Americas.

A forest of masts jutted up from the gray fog overlaying the river. The wind whipped the rigging about, filling the air with a cacophony of pinging noise that warred with the shrill of whistles and the clanging peal of bells as the lighters, the small cargo boats that ferried loads between the docks and the massive ships, worked by lantern light.

Few street lamps were to be found in this part of the city. Once erected and lighted, the lamps became targets for drunken sailors and roving bands of homeless children who pilfered goods from the warehouses. The light was considered risky to their business. Other boys carried lanterns around and hired out to walk paying clients from place to place; they didn't want the competition from the lamps either.

"You might be safer if you were to flag down a passing cab and return to the flat," his father suggested as they crouched in the shadows. "This could prove more dangerous than I'd believed."

"I'm not leaving you," Matt replied. *I can handle anything you can handle. I handled my mother's death far better than you did.* Even as that thought entered his mind, guilt followed, anchoring itself with pain-filled fishhooks.

"And I don't need a bloody handicap holding me back."

Feeling as though he'd been slapped, Matt bit back a sharp retort.

Moisture shimmered in Lord Brockton's bloodshot gray eyes. "Forgive me, Matthew. I didn't mean to say that. I'm just so tired, and now with Mr. Peabody's message, I know I'm so close to the culmination of the journey I began those seven years ago."

"Who is Mr. Peabody?" Matt asked.

Lord Brockton waved, looking anxiously back

out at the river. "A man I sometimes employ. A man of many talents and a way of finding out any number of things. He snitches for Scotland Yard upon occasion. I daresay your young friend Emma's father knows of the man."

Edmund Sharpe, Emma's father, held a position as a chief inspector in Scotland Yard.

"What did you employ Mr. Peabody to do?" Matt asked.

"He sells me bits and pieces of information," Lord Brockton explained. "This evening, Mr. Peabody brought me information about a very special shipment coming into London. We'll find it down there, my boy. On a ship called *Saucy Lass*."

"What's in the shipment?"

"I don't know," Lord Brockton admitted. "I only know that it is of interest to Lucius Creighdor." And without another word he was off, trotting toward Parson's Stairs down on the waterline.

As fast as Matt was, he had trouble catching up to his father. They raced east along the north bank of the river. Lord Brockton moved like a wraith through the white-gray fog, avoiding the few tired stevedores and sailors who had finally managed to call an end to their day.

Matt and his father stopped at length behind a stack of cargo near a dark ship sitting at anchor. It was a ketch, a two-masted cargo vessel used to run fast and hard across the ocean.

As Matt watched with heart pounding, a wagon approached and came to a stop on the dock near the ketch. A canvas sheet covered the wagonbed. The men on the wagon were silent and hard-faced. Other men joined them from the dock's shadows.

A lantern light swept the bank from an approaching barge. Running lanterns, hanging from the barge's side so that other ships wouldn't sail into it, provided enough illumination to read the ketch's name on her portside bow.

Saucy Lass.

"Do you see a flag aboard her, my boy?" his father asked.

Matt saw the fluttering rectangle high in the stern ratlines. "I see a flag, but I can't make it out." Nothing moved on her deck.

"Pity. Though I can probably get her home port from a customs house purser cheaply enough. The people we're tracking live on lies and subterfuge."

"What people, Father?"

Lord Brockton nodded toward the group standing by the wagon. "Those men. They're hellish creatures. Every last one of them. Murderous thieves and worse. But you'll never smell the stink of sulfur on them. They've made certain of that."

One of the men on the wagon lit a lantern and waved it.

Lanterns aboard the ketch also flared to life, then settled into a steady glow. At the signal, sailors came from belowdecks and stood on the ketch's deck.

Matt was ready to leave. Whatever was going on, they were definitely outmatched. Surely his father would realize that. But when he looked, Matt saw that Lord Brockton was creeping even closer to the mysterious ship and wagon.

Matt crept behind his father, both of them staying low to the muddy ground behind the crates, barrels, and bags of goods waiting to be loaded. Several times in the past Matt had gone with his father to take a deer, and there were other occasions when they'd gone dove and pheasant hunting. The way his father moved now reminded him of those times.

Now and again one of the lanterns carried by the men on the ketch threatened the shadows that cloaked the pair in the safety of the night.

The man who commanded the others aboard the ship was tall and built slim. There was a unique style in the smooth, gliding way he moved, almost like a dancer. Black clothing rendered him nearly a shadow in the night, and the drifting fog made him seem to appear and disappear, to flicker in and out of sight. The other men moved quickly at his every order, and Matt knew that part of that haste was out of fear.

"Josiah Scanlon," Lord Brockton whispered.

Hatred stained his words. "I'd hoped to catch Creighdor here tonight. But Scanlon will do for a start. Yes, indeed he will."

"Who is he, Father?" Matt asked.

"One of the men who murdered your poor mother," Lord Brockton whispered. "My precious, sweet Angeline, who never would have hurt anyone."

The answer battered Matt's senses. Struggling to maintain control, he stared at Scanlon, willing himself to see the truth of his father's accusation.

Aboard the ketch sailors used a block-and-tackle assembly to haul a canvas-wrapped object from below deck. Once they had the load in the air, they lowered it over the side to the waiting wagonbed.

One of the big men accompanying the wagon stepped forward. Lamplight glittered on the blade of a long knife he used to cut the ropes binding the canvas around the cargo.

As soon as the ropes parted, two other men stepped forward and pulled the canvas back, revealing a rectangular crate.

A thin man crossed the docks and strode up next to the ship. Scanlon moved to meet him.

The two men greeted each other in the French manner, kissing each other on both cheeks, then stepped back. They spoke in low, rapid, guttural voices.

Scanlon waved at the crate. With a lithe leap he jumped onto the back of the wagon, approached the crate, and in an incredible show of strength tore the lid of the crate free.

At first Matt thought the lid must have been merely resting on top of the crate. But the screech of nails pulling free let him know that hadn't been the case.

A scent of death, mixed with strong chemicals that put Matt in the mind of an apothecary's shop, filled the air. The odor was pungent enough to be smelled even over the other stinks rising from the river.

What looked like a dead man lay inside on a pile of straw. The shadows were too deep to clearly make out any real details. But Matt was certain he was looking at the body of a dead man.

Whoever it was, Matt knew, hadn't died recently.

"Josiah Scanlon!" Lord Brockton thundered.

Still standing aboard the wagon, making no effort to take cover, Scanlon looked in Lord Brockton's direction. "What do you want?" he asked in English.

Some of the men swung their lanterns toward the sound of Lord Brockton's voice.

Standing up from behind the hogsheads of sugar where he'd taken cover, Lord Brockton leveled a flintlock pistol and held the weapon with unwavering ferocity.

God help us, Matt thought. *He's brought a pistol.*

Worse than that, Lord Brockton looked fully

prepared to use it. Thus far in his madness, Roger Hunter had never killed anyone.

"I want you dead, Scanlon," Lord Brockton shouted, "for crimes against my country, and for the murder of my wife, God rest her soul."

"Do you dare to—" Scanlon didn't get any further. The sharp report of the pistol cut him off.

Gray smoke boiled up from the weapon as it fired, spreading out a good ten feet and mixing with the fog layers. Sparks flamed a yard from the octagonal barrel.

Sick with the horror of the murder he was certain he'd just witnessed, Matt watched Josiah Scanlon stagger back atop the wagon.

Incredibly, Scanlon looked down at his chest as if merely irritated. He brushed at orange embers that clung to the fabric of his coat.

As fearful as he was of hanging alongside his father for murder, Matt was dumbfounded to see that Scanlon was not dead. He didn't know how that could be. His father's shot had struck the man squarely.

The report of the firearm drew excited yells and questions from the nearby ships. Lanterns swung in the wagon's direction.

The light lifted Scanlon's features from the darkness, revealing a handsome, bearded face. "Get that man!" he ordered. "I want his name, and I want him dead!"

The men around the wagon rushed toward Lord Brockton, who drew another pistol from beneath his coat. But it was only one more weapon and there were more than twenty men.

Knowing his father would be overwhelmed in an instant, Matt glanced at the hogshead barrels he stood by. All of them were stacked precariously, blocked into place by wooden chocks as they lay on their sides.

Time spent hunting and fishing with his father and Finsterwald had trained Matt in the skills of a good hunter, and close calls with Gabriel through London's nights had taught Matt how to improvise during a bad situation. Violent fights with sailors and longshoremen had educated Matt in barroom brawls, boxing, and wrestling. Those lessons—like strike first and hard—had been painful, but he had learned them.

He stepped forward, gripped the chock holding the end barrel in place, and yanked with all his strength. At first he didn't think the chock would move, but then, with a loud rasp, the wooden block slid.

The bottom barrel rocked a bit, then rolled free, propelled by the weight of others stacked atop it. A crescendo of thunder followed as the hogsheads started an avalanche toward the approaching men.

"Father!" Matt yelled, certain his voice was going to be lost amid the rumble of the tumbling barrels.

The first slammed into the man leading the

rush. He didn't seem to register the threat even as the four-hundred-pound barrel rolled over him, breaking his legs and probably crushing the life from him. Two other men went down in quick succession.

Still rolling, cutting through the thick mud of the bank, the barrels continued toward the wagon, slamming up against the vehicle, driving the wagon before them, then spooking the horses into a run. Scanlon yelled at the driver, but the animals were beyond his control and his shouts and whip went unheeded.

Matt caught one last glimpse of Scanlon, who then fell forward, sprawling over the dead body in the crate. Gathering himself, watching as the men regrouped themselves after the barrels had passed, Matt sprinted toward his father.

He caught him by the arm and pulled him into motion, heading up the bank and north toward the city proper. They could hide there if they could only gain enough distance between their pursuers and themselves.

"Let me go!" Lord Brockton yelled. He flailed against Matt. His hair blew wild. He'd lost his top hat. Madness gleamed in his bloodshot eyes.

Matt didn't release his grip, dragging his father up the embankment. "You shot him, Father. Straight through the heart. I swear. I saw it."

They pounded down Nightingale Lane, but the men behind them slowly closed the distance.

By some miracle they reached the street. A clatter to Matt's left drew his attention to the hansom cab coming toward them.

Lord Brockton turned, already charging his spent pistol with powder and shot while on the run, holding the other pistol tucked under his arm. He was a seasoned veteran of the bloody Crimean War. He didn't look at the work his hands did, and Matt saw that his father's attention was directed at the group of men racing after them.

"Go," Lord Brockton said. "I've two shots now. I can kill two of them and hold the others off long enough for you to escape."

"No," Matt said. "We're both getting out of here. Together. I'm not going to leave you."

"I don't want you to die, my boy. I never should have brought you into this. I should have kept tonight's foray my secret as I have so many times in the past."

Matt stepped forward and waved. "Driver! Driver! Over here!"

Standing at the back of his carriage, a driver pulled his horse toward the street side. "'Ello, young sir. An' where might you be bound for this—" He stopped and his eyes widened. "Bloody 'ell, mate, an' w'at's this 'ere all abou'?"

"Thieves," Matt answered, reaching up and throwing wide the door. His father's evening dress and his own, so conspicuous on the docks, would now lend weight to his story. "They jumped us as we were checking on one of our investments." It was a likely enough story. He hurried up into the carriage, feeling it rock under his weight. Inside, he turned and looked at his father. "Come on."

Lord Brockton hesitated only a moment, allowing their pursuers to gain another step or three.

The cab started forward as the driver yelled to the horse.

Twisting in his seat, Matt peered back at Scanlon's men. Despite the fact that the horse-drawn cab was swiftly outdistancing them now, the men continued to follow, grim flitting shadows mixing in with the night fog.

"Weepin' Mary, Mother of God," the driver called down hoarsely. Then he screamed, a bloodcurdling sound that echoed along the street.

Startled, Matt shoved his head out the window and looked back.

The driver fought with a winged nightmare: A gargoyle with fangs and bull's horns, pasty gray skin, a lizard's tail, and backward-bending goat's legs.

But gargoyles, Matt's whirling mind insisted, were only decorations. They sat on building rooftops throughout London and caught rainwater.

They weren't *alive*.

Wings beating the air, the gargoyle raked

razor-sharp claws across the driver's face. The man's screams ended with a bubbling, liquid abruptness that left no doubt about his condition.

Without apparent effort, the monster clutched the deceased driver by one shoulder and flung the corpse away, then turned its attention to the cab.

Matt locked eyes with the foul creature, but saw nothing remotely human within the blank, silvery depths. The carved stone face remained cold and implacable, without any hint of emotion.

Moving with the speed of a striking snake, the gargoyle threw its claws at Matt's face.

Twisting and turning, Matt avoided the knife-like talons. Still, they came close enough to shear a lock of hair from his head before he could pull back into the cab. Then the cab's roof cracked. He glanced up as a stone fist punched through the lacquered wood.

The fist yanked back, tearing a huge hole in the roof. Leaning forward, the gargoyle thrust its face into the cab's interior.

Lord Brockton shoved the muzzle of his flint-lock pistol between the gargoyle's eyes and pulled the trigger. Trapped inside the cab, Matt was deafened by the pistol detonation.

The large-caliber ball crashed through the hideous face, shattering stone and ripping out the back of its head. Instead of flesh and blood— which would have been just as unlikely as what

he saw, or stone, which Matt might have expected from the gargoyle's architectural nature—a
mass of copper wires and small metal boxes
hung down from the thing's destroyed neck and
chest cavity.

"It's an automaton," Lord Brockton said. But
even that—if true—made the creature no less
amazing.

The cab bounced across a bad patch of street,
jarring so violently that the gargoyle slid free of
the roof and fell. The thing smashed into the
street and shattered. The copper wires sparked
and flashed.

"The horse," Lord Brockton shouted to be
heard.

"I'll get him," Matt offered, knowing it was
already a miracle they were still moving. He
pushed open the door and started to clamber out.

"Here," his father called, thrusting one of the
flintlocks out at him. "I'll recharge the other."

Matt hesitated only a heartbeat, then seized
the pistol and swung around to the driver's platform behind the cab. Thankfully, the reins still
lay across the top of the cab. He gathered them in
one hand, keeping the pistol in the other. Then he
pulled, hoping to get the frightened horse under
control.

Wings beat the air above him.

Glancing up, already afraid of what he knew
he would find, Matt spotted another winged gargoyle swooping toward him. The creature

looked ungainly in mid-flight, and the wingspan too improbable to keep it in the air. Matt ducked and claws swiped through the air where his head had been.

Matt rose again, throwing the heavy pistol out and taking aim, leading the gargoyle as his father had taught him when hunting. Before he could pull the trigger, the cab's left wheel dropped into a pothole.

The axle snapped and the cab tilted sickeningly. Desperate, Matt threw his weight toward the cab's side coming up off the ground, hoping he could keep the vehicle upright long enough to come to a stop.

Instead, the cab kept coming up, toppling over on its side.

Thrown clear, Matt hit the cobblestones with bruising force and rolled, dimly aware that the vehicle had fallen over and come apart only a little farther ahead. The horse dropped as though shot.

Horrified by the wreckage that remained of the cab, knowing that his father might be trapped and injured somewhere in the middle of the debris, Matt forced himself to his feet. Above, the gargoyle streaked for the wreckage of the hack as Lord Brockton stood.

"Father!" Matt yelled in warning. Fear pounded at his temples and dried his throat.

Disoriented from the wreck, Lord Brockton turned, not seeing the gargoyle.

Breathing out, trying not to think that his

father's life depended on his shooting skill, Matt let out his breath as he'd been taught, then squeezed the trigger.

BLAM!

Black smoke obscured Matt's view for a moment, looking gray against the night. Then he ran through the cloud, seeing that he had struck the gargoyle in the head. Out of control, the creature missed Lord Brockton by only inches and smashed against the wreckage of the carriage.

Exhibiting amazing calm, Lord Brockton blew down the barrel of the flintlock he held. He poured a full measure of powder into the barrel from the magazine horn he carried in his coat pocket, spat a lead ball from his mouth into the barrel, then tamped the ball and the charge into place with the ramrod.

Lord Brockton handed the charged weapon to Matt and took the empty one. "Do you see any more of those things?" He reloaded automatically.

Matt gazed into the night sky. The pistol in his hand didn't make him feel any more certain of himself. They'd barely escaped death. "No. What were they? How could they move like that? They weren't alive, were they?"

"Why don't we talk back at my flat," Lord Brockton said. "We'll have time and privacy there. And I'll tell you all of the matter concerning Lucius Creighdor as I know it. The story will be frustrating for you, my boy, because there is still so much I don't know about this most evil of men."

Chapter 2

Mind filled with questions, Matt absently gazed around the neighborhood. The flat his father kept in London was in Piccadilly. Even at this late hour, a few people still remained active in coffeehouses or drinking in favorite pubs while doing business and exchanging the news of the day.

"Come on, my boy." Lord Brockton put an arm around Matt's shoulders and guided him into the Chatsworth Building.

Kilmer, the obese night clerk at the building, sat behind the ancient desk in the room that seemed too small for him. He glanced up over his glasses as Lord Brockton and Matt entered.

"E'enin', Lord Brockton," Kilmer said in his low and steady voice. Like the clothing he wore, the old man was rumpled and faded, having obviously seen better days.

"Good evening, Mr. Kilmer," Lord Brockton

said. "Caught you busy at your paper, did we?"

"Aye sir," Kilmer replied. "You know me an' readin', Lord Brockton. I 'ave to work at 'er powerful 'ard, but I'm steady at 'er."

Matt followed his father through the foyer into the dimly lit stairwell that led to the upstairs flats.

Lord Brockton's face firmed with grim purpose as he ushered Matt up the stairs. "This is as near as I've come to Creighdor in all these past years. Scanlon is his closest associate. And—unless I don't know the man at all—Creighdor won't let my interference tonight keep him from striking back against me somehow. We must be ever vigilant."

"What do you think Creighdor will do?" Matt asked.

Lord Brockton extended the cocked pistol into the flat, using the door as a shield as he slowly pushed through. "Perhaps only strike back at me through our financial holdings. He's certainly done that before. If he'd had his way, I would have been a pauper several times before this. But I've skills, friends, and luck that he hasn't been able to negate even through his considerable efforts."

So Father's losses weren't all the result of his madness. The information made Matt feel better. For years his father had been the butt of jokes among people who had once been friends of the family.

Lord Brockton took a box of lucifers from his

coat pocket and used one of the matches to light the lantern hanging on the wall inside the room. Once the wick had taken and the light was strong, they made a quick inspection of the place.

The dwelling was a small two-bedroom flat. There was no kitchen, since meals were generally prepared downstairs and served in a common meeting room, although they could be ordered up as well. But there was a tiny pantry built into one of the sitting room walls. The sitting room held a large couch, a small table, and four chairs. The furniture was jammed into the room around the fireplace, which shared a stone chimney with the rest of the building.

Lord Brockton produced another key and opened the pantry. "Are you hungry, Matthew? As I recall, it seems you are always ravenous. I have bread and cheese and a few apples."

"No," Matthew said. "We ate only a short time ago." For a moment he feared that part of his father's madness—at least the forgetfulness—was real.

"I know we only ate a short time ago. I also know that this past hour has turned out very vigorous. I thought you might want something to keep your strength up."

Matt paced the room, thousands of questions buzzing like bees through his head. "You were going to tell me about Mother." *About her death.* He couldn't bring himself to say that, though.

Lord Brockton's eyes filled with sorrow. Then

he took a decanter and two glasses from the pantry. "Yes, I'll talk to you of your dear, departed mother, my boy. But we'll talk of her as men. Your mother deserved no less, and men will be needed to bring her murderers to justice. Perhaps I have been solitary for too long in this. But to involve another?" He shook his head. "I did not want to endanger another's life as I had your mother's. And I have seen still yet others lost to Creighdor's machinations." He gestured at Matt with an empty glass. "Yet here you are all the same."

"Sir," Matt said, "you've never been alone. I would have gladly stood at your side." *What about the times when you thought him mad, Matt? Would you have stood by him then? You didn't even try to stay home to watch over him.* He knew he couldn't lie to himself, and he didn't even try. His words were for his father's ears now.

"Make us a fire, then, my boy, while I pour us a dram."

Actually grateful for something to do—anything to feel like he was being productive—Matt knelt down to the stone fireplace. Split rounds were already laid in the hearth. He took out kindling from the nearby pot and used a lucifer to ignite the wood shavings and paper, then watched as the flames licked up onto the wood.

"Ah, now there's a cheery little blaze," Lord Brockton complimented with real fondness. However, the elation never reached his eyes.

Matt took the glass of scotch his father handed him.

Lord Brockton raised his drink. "Your mother's memory, my boy. Never one truer or fairer."

Matt lifted his glass too. They drank, and the smoky taste of the liquor raced down Matt's throat, burning and making him cough.

Then Matt sat in one of the chairs beside the fireplace while his father retreated to his bedroom. Lord Brockton came back bearing a handmade book about the size of a journal, but much thicker.

"This," his father promised, "reveals as much of Lucius Creighdor's secrets as I've yet fathomed."

Matt took the leather-bound tome, surprised by the heft of it.

"And for all that book's girth, I've found out precious little about the man," Lord Brockton admitted. "Despite the veneer of civility Creighdor puts on, he is a base villain, a wolf and a rogue, though most of his contacts among the lords and gentry would never guess at that, nor believe such without staunch evidence. That book was made by me, and it details as much of his organization and business interests as I've yet been able to discover."

Turning the pages, Matt recognized the neat, precise notations made in his father's hand. Other pages held drawings of men, ships, and symbols that made no sense to Matt.

The book also contained sepia-toned photographs of Lucius Creighdor and other men in public places. Notably, the photos had all been taken at occasions where cameras would have been accepted—during the rededication of a church, a dinner to honor a member of the House of Lords, a riding event—but there was no clue whether Lord Brockton had hired the photographer or taken the pictures himself.

The drawings and the photos all had notations under them: the date and the details of the event as well as the names of all the people. However, a number of the people surrounding Creighdor remained unidentified. Names like "Red Hat" or "One-Hand" or "Tall Man" were written under them instead.

"What you're looking at there, my boy," Lord Brockton declared, "is a man with more power than anyone in this country realizes. The sun never sets on the British Empire, they say, and with our nation's far-flung interests in the Orient, Australia, Africa, and Canada, that statement is true. But I'm also convinced that the sun never sets on Lucius Creighdor's interests either."

"You believe the man to be a criminal? A trafficker in contraband?"

"Lucius Creighdor is that and much more," Lord Brockton said. "Most know him as a wealthy man who curries favor with the Queen's courts, God save her. But Creighdor is an insidious purveyor of arcane things and a murderer as well. He is also an agent who has been sent here to overthrow the British Empire."

The accusation stunned Matt. Queen Victoria had her share of malcontents and criticizers, but as yet none of them had taken up arms against her. Disloyal talk like that could end up getting men hanged or murdered in their sleep.

"That shocks you, my boy?"

"Yes."

"You must remember, England enjoys a very prosperous place in the world. We are the foremost industrial nation. We buy raw products from all over the world, turn them into finished goods, and ship them back out for immense profits. There is no other nation capable of doing that." Lord Brockton paused. "Think of what a prize this country is, my boy, to anyone who could take it."

Matt couldn't fathom the possibility, though England had enemies throughout the world who resisted the firm hand of the Empire. "Who is Creighdor an agent of?"

"I don't know. I've been trying for years to find out. That endeavor was what took your mother and me to Canterbury seven years ago."

"You said Creighdor murdered Mother," Matthew whispered.

"Those seven years ago, I had some business dealings with a man named Mr. Horace Grape," Lord Brockton continued. "Investments in the Orient, that sort of thing. Shipping ventures as well as developing markets for English textiles.

Mr. Grape was a very progressive thinker for his time."

"I remember Mr. Grape," Matt said. "Mother liked him and his wife."

"Yes," Lord Brockton said. "He and his missus were happy and fortunate in business. Then came the day that Mr. Grape was almost financially ruined. None of his investments had paid off and he lost a fortune. During the desperate attempt he made to discover what had gone wrong, Mr. Grape found that a man had meddled in all of his affairs."

"Lucius Creighdor," Matt said.

Lord Brockton nodded. "The very same. As Mr. Grape figured afterward, Creighdor must have placed a spy among his investors. Every bargain and deal that was coming to fruition served only to line Creighdor's coffers. Finding out that truth cost Mr. Grape money and time and, at the end of the matter, he was ruined. As I have since discovered, Mr. Grape was not the only man whose life Creighdor has destroyed."

"I'd heard that Mr. Grape's losses were what caused him to shoot his wife and himself," Matt said.

"Those were lies, my boy." Pain showed in Lord Brockton's eyes. "I've never met a man more hopeful and believing in good things than Mr. Horace Grape. My hand to God on that. And Mr. Grape would never have harmed his wife."

"But you found out more."

"Yes, and I forever altered our lives, yours and mine, and saw to the undoing of your mother's." Tears sparkled in Lord Brockton's eyes. "Forgive me my weakness, Matthew. Even after all these years, such a discussion—even with you—is not . . . is not easy."

Matt tried to tell his father that he understood, but found his own throat too tight to speak. He nodded.

"I had gotten some information, from the same Mr. Peabody I met with earlier this evening, that Josiah Scanlon was in one of the old ruins around Canterbury. At that time I knew Scanlon was working with Creighdor. I decided to go and investigate. Your mother wouldn't let me go without her. You know about the ruins around Canterbury?"

"The ones left during the Roman occupation? Yes. Mr. Griswold, one of my instructors, loved Roman history. He talked about them and about Hadrian's Wall often. But I can't recall anything that would interest a businessman like Creighdor in those places."

"Nor could I," his father said. "But I do know that several men in this new field—archeology, Egyptology, whatever it's called—are in Creighdor's employ. You can also find charlatans and masters of legerdemain whom he has hired as consultants from time to time."

"Mother went to the ruins with you?"

"I persuaded her to stay at the inn where we'd

lodged outside of Canterbury. We registered under false names. That was the first time I'd ever done anything like that, though surely not the last."

"Then how did she—how did—" Matt couldn't go on.

"Scanlon," Lord Brockton answered. "You see, he and Creighdor's spies had known your mother and I were there. Scanlon went to the inn with a band of men and abducted your mother from the room while she waited on me to return from my investigation."

Matt listened in numb helplessness, almost undone for the horror he was learning of and that his father was reliving.

"At the ruins I spied on Creighdor's men and watched as they retrieved something from the dig site. I never found out what the thing was, but it was evident that whatever it was had been lost for ages. That ground hadn't been disturbed in centuries. I also saw that Creighdor's men had devices, boxes made of wires and glowing green lights that evidently helped them find what they sought."

"Boxes and wires? Like the gargoyle tonight."

"Yes. As I crept closer, Scanlon stepped out atop one of the hills. He held your mother prisoner."

"You didn't let him take her?" Matt turned cold at the possibility.

"I didn't have a choice. Scanlon told me he

would slit your mother's throat if I tried to follow them, notified the authorities, or kept poking about in his business as I had after the murder of Mr. Grape and his poor wife. I believed him. I watched helplessly as they rode away with her." Tears ran down Lord Brockton's face, openly and unashamedly. "I watched as she struggled to be free. Then—then she was gone."

Matt gazed down at his hands, amazed at the way they trembled, surprised too at the sickness in his stomach and the weakness in his legs. *How did you live through such horror, Father? For seeing that surely would have killed me.*

"Your mother was missing for a week," Lord Brockton continued in a hoarse whisper. "I thought I would go out of my mind as I waited at the inn. Perhaps I did. But on the morning of the eighth day since she had been taken, a hunter out bagging birds discovered her body. She'd been dead a day and I hadn't known." He gazed at Matt. "I let her die, Matt. God forgive me, because I know I never can forgive myself. I swear to you that I didn't know I was leaving her to die. I would have died a thousand times in her place."

Before Matt could speak, a disk of green glowing light suddenly appeared on his father's forehead. The light shifted across his father's face, elongating and pinching as it tracked the craggy features.

Fear blazed through Matt's heart. He turned, knotted his fist in his father's shirtfront, then saw the green glowing light flit down over one of Lord Brockton's eyes.

Before Matt could pull his father away from the light, something sizzled in the air between them. In that instant, his father's eye disappeared, leaving a blackened hole the size of Matt's thumb.

Slowly Lord Brockton fell forward. In a nightmarish moment, Matt saw the flames in the fireplace through his father's head.

There was no blood, only a clean, empty hole and the smell of burnt flesh.

"Father!" Matt yelled even though he knew he couldn't have survived such a wound. And then he noticed the green glowing light had settled over his own heart.

Abandoning his father's body, Matt threw himself to one side. A small, farthing-sized hole burned into the wall behind where he had been sitting.

Matt allowed himself only one more glance at his father. There was no doubt Lord Brockton was dead. Matt threw himself to the side again. He scrambled on his knees and elbows, keeping his head low, as three other burned spots appeared on the floor and walls around him.

Just as Matt reached the door, glass shattered behind him. When he looked—one frozen instant as he opened the door—he saw a winged shape at the window.

A gargoyle!

There was no doubt. The fiendish monstrosity cloaked in shadows could be nothing else. The creature gripped the stonework of the wall by the window with a rasp of claws that echoed inside the flat. It drew back its arms and threw something inside the room through the shattered window.

Matt caught a glimpse of a cylinder with red and blue sparks swirling across the top. Then he hurried through the door. In two long strides he reached the stairwell. His boots thudded against the steps.

The explosion from the flat knocked him from his feet and into the wall ahead of him before the detonation rang in his ears. Smoke filled the stairwell and descended to the lower floors in a rush. Even in the stairwell, Matt felt the heat of the fire above. The flat was on fire and the blaze was spreading.

Father!

Mr. Kilmer met Matt at the bottom of the stairs.

"'Ere now, laddie. Let's 'ave a look at ye." Concern marked the man's florid face as he brushed at embers that clung to Matt's clothing. "Where's yer father? That blast up an' sounded like a cannon, it did, an' like it come from yer—"

He stopped in mid-sentence and stiffened. One hand clutched his heart.

"Mr. Kilmer!" Matt yelled, but knew the man couldn't hear him. Fire chewed into Kilmer's clothing around the neat, circular wound in his chest.

Kilmer fell against Matt, who caught the dead man in his arms. A shadow moved in the lobby behind them.

Galvanized into action, Matt dropped Kilmer's body, turned, and raced back up the stairs to the second floor, then into the hallway. He aimed himself at the raised window that let out onto the alley opposite Hanover Park, leaping through rather than climbing. He hit the ground hard but immediately got to his feet.

Staying to the shadows, Matt ran. Paul Chadwick-Standish lived in Chelsea. Once Matt got there, he knew Paul would take him in. Whether his good friend believed the story he would tell him was another matter.

Matt ran though his heart thumped harshly in his chest and his smoke-stained breath burned the back of his throat. Tears of frustrated rage and pain poured down his face. Although he didn't yet know how he was going to achieve the goal, Matt knew he was going to find out Lucius Creighdor's deepest secrets.

Then he was going to kill the man.

Chapter 3

Paul." Matt stood outside the Chadwick-Standish family home back on the corner of Vauxhall Bridge Road and Dorset Street, only a short distance from the Thames River. He had run most of the three miles from Piccadilly, and he was out of breath.

Fog curled in around the Vauxhall Bridge. Boats and ships moved cautiously out on the dark water. Hansom cabs and carriages went in both directions along the bridge. It seemed that London never truly slept these days. Even the night had claimed a section of the city's inhabitants for its own.

"*Paul.*" Feeling more desperate, Matt felt around on the ground and found a few pebbles and small chunks of brick.

The house was old, large, and rambling compared to its newer neighbors. According to Paul, the house had been in his family for almost two hundred years, with several remodeling and refurbishing jobs during that time. The Chadwick-Standish fortune was very old, and though the family spent considerable amounts grooming and indulging itself, the fortune still grew.

Taking care to stand in the shadows that filled the alley next to the house, well out of the glare of the gaslight lamp that stood out on Vauxhall Bridge Road, Matt tossed a pebble against the second-floor window. The flat crack of stone against glass sounded almost as loud as a pistol shot to his ears.

After the fourth pebble, a shadow moved on the other side of the glass. Paul Chadwick-Standish, his thick mop of red hair unruly from sleep, leaned on the window sill.

"Do you know what time it is?" Paul smothered a bored yawn with one hand. At seventeen, only a few months older than Matt, he had perfected the appearance of indolence and boredom. But he'd also spent considerable time with his studies that Matt had not. Paul was one of the smartest and most able people Matt knew when it came to business and manners. If Matt had cared about those things, as Paul did, it might have been intimidating. Despite, or perhaps because of, their differences of opinions, they remained close friends.

"It's my father." Matt's voice seized up and he had to struggle to continue to speak. "He's dead, Paul."

Paul's face softened. "I shall let the servants know to expect you round front."

"I'm going to need an alibi for tonight," Matt explained. "I'd rather the servants not know what time I arrived."

"Round back with you, then." Paul gestured toward the rear of the house and was gone from the window in a moment.

Matt made his way to the back of the large house. He had barely arrived before Paul opened the back door and allowed him entrance.

"Quickly," Paul whispered. "You know Estelle is a frightful old biddy and kowtows to my mother's every whim."

He led the way through the darkened house without the aid of a light, one of his hands knotted in Matt's shirtsleeve to guide him.

Inside his upstairs bedroom, Paul wrinkled his nose in distaste. "You reek of smoke."

"There was a fire."

"A fire?" Paul arched his brow and took a seat in the large, overstuffed chair at the foot of the impossibly huge bed. He let his sock-clad feet dangle over the chair's arm while he knitted his fingers together before him.

"Or it could be from the explosion," Matt guessed.

"An explosion as well?" Paul's eyebrows lifted.

Matt walked to the window and peered out. "I have to tell you, Paul. There will be an investigation into this matter."

"Burning and exploding buildings in Piccadilly," Paul commented. "I should hope there would be an investigation. A quite lengthy one at that."

"And," Matt said heavily, "my father's death will probably draw the Scotland Yard inspectors after me. Eventually, they'll come to your door."

"What do you need me to do?"

Hesitating only a little, Matt said, "If you're ever asked, swear that I was with you tonight. The word of two sons of English lords will carry weight."

Paul spread his hands. "Of course. Whatever you need."

"Things may go badly for you, Paul. This thing that I'm facing—that *we're* facing—is huge. What do you know of a man named Lucius Creighdor?"

Paul waved nonchalantly. "I've met him at social gatherings. Parties. Balls given by the Queen." He paused, focusing on Matt. "Lucius Creighdor is a cunning man who covets a seat in the House of Lords. Over the last few years he has increased his financial empire here and abroad. But he's not titled. He's a hanger-on at court, always soliciting the good will of the other lords and paying attention to the ladies. Especially the widowed and childless ones who might be able to bequeath him a title by proxy. I've also heard his name mentioned in blackmail schemes against some lords to get them to use the influence to help his own ends." He paused. "Why do you want to know about Lucius Creighdor?"

"Because he's the man responsible for my father's murder and very nearly my own," Matt said, then hesitated. "If I get you involved in this, I am to blame."

"If these people killed your father and tried to hurt you," Paul replied flatly. "I'm already involved. Now, please tell me what really happened so that we can figure out our best lies."

"You realize, of course," Paul said finally, after Matt finished recounting the night's events, "that the greatest threat here is not inspectors from Scotland Yard. The greatest threat—"

"Is Creighdor," Matt said, growing impatient.

Paul lifted a forefinger and locked eyes with Matt. "No. It would be an unfortunate mistake to think that. Possibly even a fatal mistake, given Creighdor's proclivity for violence. The greatest threat lies in your own lack of understanding of your adversary."

Matt blew out his breath in exasperation. "Creighdor's a murderer. What else is there to understand?"

"Firstly, I must ask you if you know with absolute certainty—and please pardon my bluntness in this matter—whether Mr. Lucius Creighdor, friend to the crown of England, is even guilty of murdering your father?"

Matt thought about that, knowing Paul was in the habit of setting traps for him when they planned together.

"You did not see Creighdor at the flat in Piccadilly," Paul pointed out. "Nor did you hear him give orders to kill your father or you."

Matt let out a tense breath, knowing that Paul was right.

"And that was in spite of the fact that, according to your own testimony, young Lord Brockton, your father tried his level best to shoot Mr. Josiah Scanlon to death in cold blood."

"'Young Lord Brockton'?" Matt repeated.

Paul steeped his fingers beneath his chin with the forefingers resting in the cleft. "Yes. With your father removed from this mortal coil, doubtless you will assume his mantle and ancestral title. Which, I might at this moment point out, some could possibly think would give you sufficient motive to take your father's life."

"I would never—"

Paul held up a hand to cut off Matt's angry retort. "No. I would never think such a thing. I know you loved your father in spite of your estrangement from him. But many people, Matt, don't know you as I do."

"All right," Matt acquiesced.

"I think your father could possibly have had much about Creighdor and his situation correct. However, what he did *not* know got him—and very nearly you—killed tonight." Paul shrugged. "Your father didn't know enough about his enemy. Even after seven years. You can't deal with that lack and hope to emerge alive. Nor do you have seven years in which to learn about your enemy."

"You make the task sound impossible."

"Quite." Paul bared a mirthless grin. "Or, at least, it would be. If you weren't my friend and I weren't prepared to go the distance for you. But you are, and I am."

Matt waited. That was the best way to deal with Paul while he was thinking aloud. Paul had always had an interest in business and a knack for solving problems. He'd already started investing in cargoes, making small profits, then pushing them back into more investments for larger profits. With the way he was going, he would be independently wealthy within a few years.

"I remain unconvinced as to whether Scanlon is a creature of Creighdor's or whether the reverse is true," Paul said. "But let's examine why you were allowed to escape that flat unscathed."

"'Allowed'?" Matt couldn't believe he'd heard correctly. "I wasn't *allowed*, Paul. Whoever killed my father was trying to kill me."

"Whoever it was succeeded in murdering Mr. Kilmer as well. Yet you escaped from that flat and from that building. I suggest that perhaps you were allowed to escape."

"They killed my father. They meant to kill me."

"We can't afford to let ourselves believe that if we're to confront these men. You were allowed your freedom for a reason. We must ferret out what that reason might be." Paul rubbed his hands together, then pushed up from the chair and crossed over to the fireplace.

Matt watched his friend and couldn't help but wonder at his own success in escaping the flat.

"Scanlon and Creighdor need you alive for a reason." The glow of the flames painted Paul's lean frame golden against the darkness that filled the bedroom.

"My father knew more about their evil intentions than I do. What could I possibly know that he didn't know?"

"I imagine he simply knew too much. Your father, Matt, was not a man to let things be once he sank his teeth into something." Paul glanced at Matt from the fireplace. He spoke in lower, more respectful tones. "Your father, unlike my own, was a true hero, Matt. He fought in the Crimean War, and he earned his honors, though he seldom leaned on them no matter how badly things went. He was a man who deserved so much more than this mean life he'd been treated to since the death of your mother."

Pride, followed immediately by a strong sense of loss, echoed within Matt. He felt shamed that he'd ever thought less of his father than Paul apparently had. But he'd had his own experiences with the man that his friend hadn't. Missed birthdays, long unexplained absences, and the periods of feeling like an unwelcome guest around his father had all built a thick barrier of resentment and pain.

"Why didn't you go to the police to let them know your father was murdered?" Paul asked.

"Because no one would believe me. Especially not when I told them about the gargoyle automaton that attacked the hansom cab and killed the driver. You had trouble believing me."

"Agreed. So at the very least, if you told the police, they would think you mad and very probably have you locked up. Many people believe that insanity is hereditary."

"Creighdor knew I couldn't go to the police," Matt said.

"If you were in police custody, he would eventually have access to you."

"You believe they could have captured me."

"Yet they chose not to. I find that highly intriguing."

"Assuming, of course, that you are right about them letting me go and I didn't simply escape on my own." Matt still found it hard to believe—and, indeed, did not want to believe—that his escape was a callous and shrewd allowance.

Paul smiled. "I don't wish to take anything away from your own resourcefulness, Matt. I've seen your abilities displayed during several of our adventures out amid London's rougher areas to know you can handle yourself in violent times. Please don't get me wrong. It could be you escaped on your own. If so, that avenue needs no further exploration. You know that you are a fugitive from Creighdor and Scanlon. I choose to illuminate other possibilities so we may be prepared to handle whatever comes our way."

Matt understood. He relaxed a little more, feeling certain that Paul could catch anything he might overlook. Thinking he was allowed his escape deeply disturbed him and undermined his confidence.

"Don't underestimate your situation, Matt," Paul cautioned. "Scanlon and Creighdor haven't seen the true nature of the danger that you present them. If they set you loose, they believe they set free a mouse that ran for safety."

"I was a mouse. I did run for safety."

Paul shook his head. "If you had, you would never have mentioned any of this to me. No, you're a thinking threat to them. They just haven't realized it yet. But they will."

Matt felt redeemed at that.

"Wipe that smile from your face. That wasn't intended as a compliment."

"Perhaps," Matt said grimly, "but I'll take it as such. Those men killed my father, Paul. They haven't yet learned anything of me or the lengths to which I'm willing to go."

Paul nodded slightly. "In letting you go, they

revealed something more of themselves than you have noticed."

Matt turned Paul's statement over in his mind but couldn't make sense of it. He knew, though, that his friend's keen mind had seized on something. "What did they reveal?"

"If they had been totally in control of the situation, they would never have let you go. No, they gambled that your freedom would benefit them in some way. Or would get them something they couldn't get on their own. They have revealed that they possess a vulnerability."

"What vulnerability?"

"We have yet to discover that." Paul turned and took up a slim walking stick that he often carried. He gave it a quick twist that revealed the wickedly keen blade disguised within. "But we will."

The sound of knocking on the door of the guest bedroom in the Chadwick-Standish home drew Matt from an uneasy slumber. He'd spent the remnant of the night among violent phantoms drawn from memory and from nightmare.

Sitting upright in the bed, Matt called, "Who is it?"

"Paul." A faint hint of urgency sounded in his voice. Few would have noticed it.

"Come in." Matt slung his legs from the bed, leaving the warmth of the covers and feeling the chill that hugged the room.

Paul entered. He was dressed for the day in a custom-made dark suit that fit his rapier-thin frame well. He carried his trick walking stick. A ruffled tie stood out at his neck. His red hair was carefully combed, his side whiskers neatly in place and his thin mustache waxed so that it was a little more noticeable.

"You have a visitor," Paul declared.

"I do?"

"Yes. A most interesting man. I've had the somewhat dubious pleasure of entertaining him for the last few minutes in the drawing room. He's an inspector from Scotland Yard."

"Inspector."

"Yes. So he says. I shall, of course, ascertain the veracity of his statements before we accompany him."

"He wants us to accompany him?" Matt struggled to catch up. His thoughts raced.

"Not us. *You.*" Paul lifted his walking stick and crossed his arms. "I expect you to summarily reject his offer, no matter how heavy-handed he becomes. After all, you are the son of a British war hero and a lord. He can't handle you the way he would the usual low-browed ruffian lot that he's obviously more at ease dealing with."

"Accompany him where?"

"Please get dressed," Paul said. "Making a commoner wait, even one from Scotland Yard, is permitted and even expected. But if we tarry too long, our dear inspector might get it into his

45

mind that we are concocting something." He smiled. "Instead of surmising that we were up half the night at it."

Scotland Yard Inspector George Donovan stood to greet Matt as Paul ushered him into the drawing room. He was a tall man, built wide and strong as a stevedore. His jaw was a slab, a hard-angled finish to a head that looked like it had been formed from a well bucket. His haircut was obviously fresh, still showing white around his forehead, ears, and neck where the sun hadn't yet tanned the skin. His mustache remained thick and bushy, obviously a source of pride to him. His clothes were new but didn't quite fit him. He was in his mid- to late thirties.

"Mr. Hunter," Paul said offhandedly, "this is Inspector George Donovan of Scotland Yard."

Donovan smiled, but the bleak effort never touched his dark, suspicious eyes. He offered his hand. "Good morning, Lord Brockton. Pleased to mee'cher."

Matt took the man's hand, feeling the rough calluses against his own palm. The inspector was evidently a man used to hard labor. His knuckles felt knobby and prominent.

"You don't address me as Lord Brockton," Matt corrected in a neutral voice. His throat felt tight with emotion but he kept that inside. "My father holds that title. I am Master Brockton, if you insist on formality. However, I don't stand on title that often, Inspector. You may address me as Mr. Hunter."

"Very well," Donovan said.

Matt knew Paul had chosen to stand far enough away that the inspector would have to constantly turn his head to address them both. And seeing as how they were both the sons of lords, Donovan had to address them in a polite manner.

Matt pointed to the nearby couch. "Please sit."

Donovan hesitated a moment, clearly not liking the idea of being ordered around by someone he'd come to investigate, much less someone probably half his age and young enough to be his son. He sat on the edge of the couch and held his bowler hat in his hands.

"Now, Inspector," Matt said, working hard to manage a light tone, "Mr. Chadwick-Standish tells me you took time out of your busy day to come here in search of me."

"Yes, I did. Would you mind telling me your whereabouts last night, Mr. Hunter?"

Matt acted surprised that such a question would be asked. "I stayed here as Mr. Chadwick-Standish's guest as I have on a number of occasions," he said. Then he asked, "Why?" because such a question was normal under any circumstances. Still, his heart thudded inside his chest.

Donovan switched his attention to Paul. "Could you verify that, Mr. Chadwick-Standish?"

"That Mr. Hunter was here at this house?"

Paul looked cold and imperious and angry. He drew himself up to his full height, looking like a drawn blade.

"Yes."

"Of course I can, and I do," Paul snapped. "And with the same breath I admonish you that you've trespassed over a very delicate line, Inspector Donovan."

"A line, sir?" Donovan blinked and looked for a moment like an animal caught in a trap it did not understand.

"You've questioned the integrity and honor of the son of a lord of the Queen's court." Paul's tone was a rapier edge, straight and narrow and deadly. "More than that, you chose to do it in front of him with no regard to respect."

Donovan said gruffly, "I intended no disrespect."

"Were you of breeding instead of common stock, and were this a hundred years ago, and were it me you'd just disrespected in such a cavalier fashion, I'd have you out on a field of honor within the hour with dueling pistols."

For all his dilettante behavior, Paul carried an Old World sophistication about him. He played the joker and the wastrel to the hilt, but his values about honor never wavered.

Donovan thrust his jaw out and adjusted the set of his head again. The threat of violence didn't frighten him. "As I said, Mr. Chadwick-Standish, I intended no disrespect. But there has been . . . an occurrence that requires some haste if we are to resolve this matter."

"Which brings us to why you're here in the first place," Matt said.

"Yes, Mr. Hunter," Donovan agreed, changing his gaze to Matt. "I've come in regards to a rather unfortunate event." His dark eyes locked with Matt's. "I'm afraid that I've come with some bad news. Your father is dead."

Matt knew the police inspector stated the news bluntly like that to hurt him. The naked statement, stripped of any kind of sympathy, struck him like a blow. He felt his face break and he lost control for a moment. He sucked in a ragged breath as he closed an iron fist around his emotions.

"Mr. Hunter," Donovan said.

Matt kept himself centered and looked through the police inspector.

"Mr. Hunter."

"Inspector Donovan," Paul interrupted, coming over to Matt's side, "have you not a shred of decency? You've just told Mr. Hunter his father is dead. Perhaps you might give him a moment to gather his thoughts."

Donovan frowned but said nothing.

After a moment, Matt asked, "What happened to my father?" He really wanted to know. Could a doctor tell that someone had burned a hole through his father's head with some unknown weapon? Might that be a fact he could exploit against Creighdor? Was his father even recognizable from the explosion?

"If you're up to it, Mr. Hunter," Donovan said, "I'd like to take you to the flat your father had in Piccadilly and discuss the matter with you there."

Everything in Matt screamed for him to refuse the inspector. He was safe in Paul's home. His reluctance to go to his father's death scene was understandable. Paul had even prepared him with the possible excuse during their conversation in the upstairs room.

But he knew he had to see the building.

"Of course, Inspector," Matt replied. He could not stay away any more than a moth could avoid a flame.

Chapter 4

The blast that had detonated within the building the night before had destroyed a large section of the second floor. Debris—broken brick, naked timbers, and plaster—lay scattered in all directions around the structure.

The accompanying fire had gutted most of the second floor. The western wall and ceiling lay in collapsed ruin, blackened and burned.

Stunned by the horror of the scene laid out before him, Matt couldn't speak.

A crowd of people ringed the site. Several of them pointed in Matt's direction. Some of them were locals and recognized him.

Inspector Donovan and Paul stepped from the carriage.

"Are you sure my father was in that?" Matt asked.

"Yes." Donovan studied Matt. "His body was taken from the second floor."

"Where is he?"

"We've got the body for now, Mr. Hunter."

"There are matters that I must attend to. His funeral—" Matt's voice broke and he couldn't go on. Only then, looking around at the people watching him, did he realize he had to see to his father's burial.

"In due time," Donovan said. His voice was softer.

"Do you—" Matt's voice broke. "Are you certain—"

"It's your father, all right. We've had a few people identify him since last night. Friends and business associates."

Two men from the nearby crowd came over. They wore suits and carried notebooks and pencils.

"Inspector Donovan, isn't it?" one of the men asked. He was tall and smooth-shaven except for a thin mustache. "I'm Nash. From the *Morning Post*. I didn't get to interview you for the first edition we put out last night, but I'd be happy to include a few words in our next edition."

Donovan hesitated only for a moment. "All right. Just make certain you spell the name right."

Matt stepped away from the Scotland Yard inspector. During his years with his father, Matt had learned to stay away from the predatory reporters from Fleet Street, London's hot spot for journalism.

Newspapers and pamphlets published as many as three and four times a day found an eager audience awaiting the latest information on Parliament, investments, and gossip about the lords and ladies. That audience wanted to know who had lost fortunes and whose marriages were in trouble. A murder, particularly of someone like Lord Brockton, who had been the subject of more than a few articles as a war hero and a potential crackpot, would sell newspaper copies.

"Inspector Donovan," Nash said, licking his pencil and putting it to paper, "could you elaborate on what you believe happened in that building?"

Donovan assumed a stance and stared in Matt's direction. "As you know, the flat most heavily damaged in the mysterious explosion that took place here last night belonged to Lord Brockton. The man has struggled with reality for some time, ever since the unexplained murder of his wife seven years ago. I've heard stories that Mr. Roger Hunter was searching for the murderers of his late wife. He'd been brought into police custody a few times for carrying weapons, and was almost sent to be examined for mental soundness."

Anger, dark and violent, stirred within Matt. He breathed out in an effort to control himself. Everything Donovan was saying, he knew, would get published. A mad lord tearing through the streets of London was interesting news. The link to his mother's unexplained murder would tantalize readers and gossipmongers.

"What I believe happened is that Lord Brockton was storing up supplies to confront the men he imagined responsible for his poor wife's death," Donovan said. "Only copious amounts of gunpowder could have caused the damage you see before you. The damage done by the explosion offers testimony as to how much he probably had stored. Obviously, in his derangement, Lord Brockton made a mistake that cost not only his life, but the lives of—"

Unable to bear it any longer, knowing that his father's name was going to be libeled in the papers and slandered on the streets for days and weeks to come, Matt turned toward Donovan and strode across the distance that separated them.

"Close your lying mouth!" Matt demanded harshly, shaking off Paul's attempt to stop him. "You don't know what happened last night! You weren't there!"

The newspaper reporters immediately turned to face Matt. Their pencils worked across the small notebooks they carried.

"Who are you?" Nash asked.

Matt ignored the man. They'd know who he was soon enough.

"Mr. Hunter," Donovan said, "I must insist that you stay out of police affairs. The truth about your father will come out and—"

Before he could stop himself, before Paul could intervene, Matt had Donovan's coat caught up in both his fists and muscled the bigger man back against the carriage, slamming him back with considerable effort.

"The truth about my father," Matt spat, shoving his face close into the police inspector's. "You don't know the truth about my father. And there is no way I'm going to stand here and listen to you tarnish him with your stupid guesswork and small, evil mind."

"Matt," Paul called, taking hold of his left elbow and pulling. "*Matt*. Let. Go." He continued to pull.

The journalists and the crowd watched in silence. Matt felt their eyes upon him. Still, he couldn't release Donovan.

"Get off of me, boy." Donovan put a big hand in Matt's face and shoved him back. "You're a cat whisker away from getting arrested for daring to put your hands on an inspector of Scotland Yard."

Reluctantly, Matt released Donovan's coat and stood a few feet away. He shook Paul off, barely hearing his friend's pleas to walk away. He pointed at Donovan. "Don't you use my father's name and his misfortune to your own advantage, Inspector. Not while I'm alive to make you regret it, and certainly not while I'm standing within reach of you."

Face red and eyes wide, Donovan dusted his

coat with his hands. "Your father," he said in a cruel voice, "was a madman. Whatever use he was to the Queen and to England vanished years ago when he allowed his wife to be killed. Or hired someone to kill her."

Paul reached for his friend, but Matt stepped cleanly through his grasping arms and fired a fist into Inspector Donovan's face.

Evidently Donovan hadn't thought Matt would dare hit him, either because he was a policeman or because he was so much bigger than Matt. Donovan realized it only a split second before Matt's fist hit its target. The inspector tried to lift his arms to defend himself, but the effort came too late.

Matt's blow split the smirk the man wore. Donovan went back and down, dropping to one knee as his eyes glazed for just a moment. Then he glared up at Matt. "You're gonna pay for that, you are." He rose from the ground much more quickly than Matt would have thought.

Hammered by Donovan's bulk, Matt hit the ground on his back and felt the larger man on top of him. Before he could escape, Donovan aimed a hard blow. Pain detonated across Matt's face. At the last instant he'd managed to turn his head so that the punch caught him on his left cheek and jaw instead of full on as Donovan had intended. Through a sheer effort of will, he made the three images of Donovan he saw become one again.

"Now you're gonna find out why a half-grown whelp shouldn't think he can bite a full-grown dog," the inspector promised as he straddled Matt's chest. He drew back his fist again.

Feeling the man's weight shift on him, Matt braced his feet and shoulders, shoving up and twisting at the same time. Caught off-guard, Donovan tumbled to one side.

Still dazed from the inspector's harsh blow, Matt rolled and got to his feet.

Donovan surged up from the ground bellowing like a wounded bull. His attack lacked finesse, planning, or real skill. He was a brawler, used to overcoming his adversaries through sheer strength and size. Matt had the advantage of having faced several such men before, and he had skills in boxing and wrestling to rely on.

Donovan jabbed twice with his left hand and circled to his right. Matt slapped the other man's jabs away with his left hand, using the limb much as he would a fencing épée. He circled with Donovan, coming around to match the man.

Donovan feinted with his left, then stepped in to bring his right fist squarely on Matt's head.

Trusting his eye and his fencing instincts, Matt shifted his left hand inside Donovan's right arm. He made jarring contact with the police inspector's inside forearm with the back of his wrist to throw the blow off target, then stepped inside.

Rolling his shoulder behind the blow as he'd been taught by small-time prizefighters down on the docks, Matt punched through Donovan's chin. The police inspector's neck jerked sideways with the force of the blow. With his hips twisted to get more from the punch, Matt easily reached beyond the big man's face as his head turned. Drawing his hand back, Matt managed to pop Donovan in the face with his elbow as he withdrew.

Staggered by the blows, Donovan wavered uncertainly for a moment.

Matt didn't know what was holding the inspector up other than sheer stubbornness. Keeping both hands up and ready, Matt circled to the right. Beyond Donovan, the crowd watched and yelled support for both fighters, as eager for blood now as they were at the public hangings at Newgate and the other prisons.

"You throw a pretty good punch for a lordling," Donovan grated. "I'll give you that." He spat blood. "But I didn't come out here today to fetch me a whipping or to be made sport of."

He wiped blood from his mouth and nose with his left hand, then reached into his coat pocket with his right hand and brought out a short fisherman's billy. Made of leather and packed tight with lead shot, the fish billy could break a man's forearms or fingers as easily as it jellied a fish's brain.

Paul started forward, twisting his walking

stick to free the sword blade hidden inside the elegant casing. His face was grim and set, and Matt had no doubts that his friend would run the police inspector through if he had to in order to stop the man.

"Mr. Donovan," a sharp feminine voice came from the crowd. "Unless you intend to see your newfound job as inspector vanish in the space of a drawn breath, I suggest you listen to me and stop your foolishness this instant."

Matt realized he knew the voice.

Donovan did too. He halted, took a deep breath and expelled it, and lowered the billy. He cursed with fervor.

"No," Matt said. "You won't use that kind of language in front of a lady." He stepped forward.

Donovan shifted the billy as he focused on Matt.

"Mr. Donovan," the female voice said again.

A tic fluttered Donovan's left eye. "Another time, lordling," he said in a voice that carried only to Matt. "Somebody already has your number. Just a matter of time."

Taking two steps back to get clear of any sudden move on Donovan's part, Matt stared at the Scotland Yard inspector. *And what does that mean?*

Before he could frame the question, Emma Sharpe stepped between him and Donovan.

Dressed in a long dark green dress that narrowed at her pinched waist and flowered into a bustle long enough to cover her feet, Emma was a sight to behold in that part of Piccadilly. Her strawberry blond hair was carefully pinned up under a high hat made festive by ribbons gathered to look like blossoms. Her shoulders were narrow and carried high, showing proper form that had been schooled into her by her mother.

Concern filled her face, but she made her tone stern when she spoke, reminding Matt of a schoolteacher. Her bright blue eyes bored into Matt's.

"And what do you think you were doing?" she demanded.

Matt drew himself up to his full height. Emma was one of his oldest and dearest friends, second only to Paul. But he wasn't going to take rebuke from a woman in front of the crowd that had gathered.

"Miss Sharpe," Matt said, "I beg your pardon for being so blunt, but this affair is none of your business."

"None of my business?" Emma put a hand to her chest, obviously aghast. Anger turned her pale face red. She had a small dusting of freckles across the bridge of her nose that made her look younger than her sixteen years.

"That's right, Miss Sharpe," Donovan growled. "This here's between us."

"So I should just leave you to bashing each other's brains out?" she asked, turning her attention to the inspector.

Donovan looked uncertain.

Paul was grinning behind the inspector. He'd learned years ago to stay out of the way when Emma got on a roll.

She brought up her parasol and jabbed at Donovan with it. "Well, if that's what you think, you're going to be sadly mistaken."

At every word, at every jab, Donovan yelped and gave ground, getting hit a few times in spite of his efforts. Matt couldn't help grinning at the man's discomfort. He'd been at the other end of Emma's quick wit and sharp tongue a few times over the years and those experiences had been anything but pleasant.

The crowd whooped and laughed at Donovan.

Nash and his fellow journalist wrote furiously.

Standing to one side, Paul gazed on in wry amusement.

Emma swung on Matt. "And you," she said, leveling her parasol and starting for him.

"Matt." Paul lifted his walking stick and tossed it to him.

Effortlessly Matt caught the walking stick, reversed his hold on it and parried Emma's parasol. She jabbed at him twice more, but he turned aside her blows and stood his ground till she was too close to jab any more and much closer than a young woman should be in public.

"Easy there," Matt said, holding the walking stick at the ready.

Emma sighed and all of the fight went out of her. That was how she had always been. Matt had never met a more levelheaded girl—and now young woman—in his life.

"I thought you were dead," she said simply.

"What?" Matt blinked, trying to understand.

"When I heard about your father's flat," Emma said, "about the way it was destroyed, I thought you were dead. You left me a note that you were going to have dinner with your father last night. I'd presumed you were together when the accident happened."

"No," Matt said, and immediately felt guilty about lying to Emma. They had agreed to attend a play she'd wanted to see. He cursed himself for not thinking that she'd be worried about him.

"Do you know what happened?" she asked.

"No." *Two lies*, Matt thought, and the bitter swell of emotion stung him. He lowered the walking stick so it was no longer between them. "Inspector Donovan found me at Paul's house and gave me the news. We had only just arrived."

"To beat each other's brains out?"

Matt felt defensive. "I took exception to something Mr. Donovan said to the press about my father."

"Mr. Donovan," Emma said, "is a brute and a bully when it comes to his job." She turned to the two journalists. "And you may quote me on that, Mr. Nash."

"Yes, miss," Nash replied, smiling broadly. "I shall plan to."

"But if you take any liberties with my statements, you could be in for a bad time of it."

"Miss?"

"What I mean is that my father, Chief Inspector Sharpe, will not like that I made a statement, but I am his daughter and can get away with more than a journalist with a bad gambling habit."

Nash took a step back, obviously caught off-balance by the veiled threat in her words. He touched the brim of his hat. "Yes, miss. I understand perfectly."

"As for yourself, Mr. Higgins," Emma said to the second journalist, "I should be careful of my step were I you. There are many in London's high society circles that should like to know the identity of the man giving Harold Darling the half-truths and outright lies he's seen fit to publish in his muckraking column these past few months."

The other man touched his hat as well. "Yes, miss."

"I would furthermore like the rest of this conversation held without busybodies, professional and amateur."

Both men excused themselves and retreated to the ranks of the amateur busybodies without protest. Even Paul took a short step away.

"There." Emma took another deep breath as

she surveyed Matt. "You are all right?" She removed a handkerchief from her small purse and touched his face, blotting away the blood.

"I am." Matt caught her gloved hand and pushed the handkerchief away.

"You should have a doctor look at your face."

"Emma, please." Matt cut his gaze over his shoulder. "There's already gossip enough in the air without you adding a few more logs."

"I'm your friend, Matt. Everyone who knows you knows that. And those who don't know you will know of our friendship soon enough." Emma gazed at him. "I'm not ashamed of that, nor do I see a reason to be."

"I didn't say that. I just don't want to see your reputation sullied." Matt caught her hand in his and squeezed it affectionately. "This thing that's happened . . . " He hesitated. "It's going to be bad. Really bad. Given my father's reputation, all kinds of vile things are going to be said. I'd rather you not be subjected to them."

Emma eyed him levelly. "That's my choice, is it not?"

"Miss Sharpe," Donovan said, approaching. His lips had swelled and one eye was nearly swollen shut.

Remembering the billy the man carried, Matt took one step and inserted himself between Emma and the police inspector.

"You're interrupting an inspector in the course of his duties, Miss Sharpe," Donovan said. "I hadn't finished questioning Mr. Hunter."

"Yes," Emma said flatly, "you have."

"Miss Sharpe, your father—"

"Is still chief at the Yard, Inspector, and will be for some time. I have my father's ear, and I shan't hesitate to use that to my advantage in this matter."

"You do me a disservice, miss."

"Did my father assign to you the investigation into Lord Brockton's death?"

Donovan didn't answer.

"No, as a matter of fact, he did not. Do you know how I know that, Inspector?"

"No, miss."

"Because after I learned of this horrible event, after I learned that the building had exploded, I asked my father to tend to this matter himself. He told me that he would. I trust my father's word implicitly."

"Yes, miss. But it wasn't just Lord Brockton what got killed in all this bother." Donovan's eyes pierced Matt. "Seven other people was killed last night as well. They've got families what will be looking for somebody to swing for this."

Seven people. The number was staggering. Matt knew about Mr. Kilmer, but who were the others? How could anyone be so callous as to murder his father and seven other innocent people? Were they all killed in the explosion?

And for *what*? What threat did his father truly pose to Creighdor and Scanlon?

"When my father discovers who took Lord Brockton's life," Emma said, "he'll know the man or men who murdered those other unfortunate souls. Unless those deaths are unconnected and all happened to occur on the same night, which I believe is highly unlikely, the same man or men perpetrated those crimes. Don't you think, Inspector?"

"Yes, miss."

"Then I suggest you get on with whatever duties my father has currently assigned you and forget about this matter." Emma looked at Matt. "Unless you'd like to prefer charges against Inspector Donovan, *Lord* Brockton."

If Donovan felt anxious in the slightest about Matt bringing charges against him, he didn't reveal it.

"No," Matt said, returning Donovan's flat-eyed stare full measure. "No, that won't be necessary. I feel that whatever recompense the inspector owed me was collected today."

Donovan touched his swollen jaw and grinned. "Says you. And I say if you're so easily satisfied, you've a lot to learn about being a man."

"That will be quite enough," Emma said.

Grinning a little lopsidedly from the swelling, the inspector found his hat, then looked at Matt. "Another time, Mr. Hunter. Another time." He turned and walked away.

"How long have you known Inspector Donovan?" Emma asked.

"Today only," Matt answered.

"There seemed to be a lot of rancorous feelings between the two of you."

Matt wondered about that, but he said, "The man has a knack for making enemies quickly."

"And that's how you view Donovan? As an enemy?"

Matt regarded her. "Would it be safe to view Donovan in any other fashion?"

After only a brief hesitation, Emma said, "No. It would not. He's a dangerous man, Matt. Not altogether trustworthy."

"Then how did your father come to name him as inspector?"

"George Donovan has picked up a little political clout and favor over the years. He's sought it out and curried it, making certain the right crimes were swept under the carpet, the right people protected for the wrong reasons." Emma sighed. "My father knows this, but he thought keeping Donovan close to hand would prove a wiser strategy than allowing him free movement."

"'Keep your friends close and your enemies closer,'" Matt said.

"A quote?"

"Yes."

"I'm afraid I don't recognize it."

"You'll not find it in one of those science books you favor as reading material," Matt said.

"It doesn't sound very nice."

"It's not," Matt said, watching Donovan disappear into the crowd around the devastated building. "It was said by a Chinese military strategist named Sun Tzu nearly five thousand years ago. He also said, 'To know your enemy, you must become your enemy.'"

"How positively dreadful."

"It seems to have a new fascination for me."

"Matt."

He looked at her.

"Tell me that you truly don't know who killed your father."

"I don't," Matt said, and that was close enough to the truth that he didn't feel too badly. "But I'm going to find out."

Chapter 5

Gabriel had only the one name. If he had a surname, or if Gabriel actually was his surname, Matt didn't know it. He also didn't know his age, which could have been anywhere from fifteen to twenty.

He stood only a few inches over five feet tall. Even at rest, nervous energy filled him, causing his knees to bounce constantly as his eyes roved over everything and everyone around him. He had a hard time sitting and usually thought best while on his feet.

Most people who talked to Gabriel got the distinct impression he wasn't listening to them, because he seldom ever watched their faces. That impression was always incorrect. Gabriel took note of every word spoken to him and also kept track of as many as two or three other conversations going on around him.

He sat at a corner table in the back of a

seedy pub on the East End. He looked even smaller in the shadows. His eyes were black as coal, made more startling because his face was wan and pale. Most of Gabriel's work didn't take place in the full light of day. His shoulder-length black hair was tied back in a queue. He wore black pants, a pale blue shirt, and a black vest. A floppy black longshoreman's hat lay on the table in front of him.

"I 'eard about your father," Gabriel said. "I offer me condolences. Never knew me own father, but I suppose losin' one is ever so 'ard. By ever' light I heard about 'im, Lord Brockton was a good man."

"Yes," Matt agreed. "He was."

"An' all them stories people want to push off on you about 'im bein' daft or round the bend, why I wouldn't listen to them, was I you, Matt." Gabriel shrugged. "Prolly a lot of rubbish an' the like in all them stories. People like to talk, they do. An' it's usually about nuffink, nuffink at all. If'n they don't know about somethin', they make up stories about it. That's why the newspapers got all them reporters workin' for 'em the way they do. For them people what can't make up stories all on their own."

"Well, and wasn't that the perfect example of brevity and tact," Paul commented sourly.

Gabriel looked at Paul and sneered. "I says what I knows to say. An' I means ever' word of it, no matter 'ow hit comes out. You got no call turnin' your nose up at me or what I do or 'ow I chooses to do it."

"You're a thief," Paul said.

"An' you're an hinvestor." Gabriel stretched the word out, turning it into something foul. "There's dockworkers what swears you an' your kind are sons of the devil 'imself. Usin' a man's back to load an' unload your ships, then throwin' 'im out in the cold when 'e's too used up an' broke down to fend for 'imself. Leastways when I empty a man's purse, I only steal from them what can put in another day's work for wages somewheres else to get more money. I don't steal from a man what can't take care of 'imself."

Paul grinned. "So I'd wager there are not a lot of people that like either of us."

Gabriel smiled back and lifted his bottle. "Proper set of rogues is what we are. Just wearin' different cuts of cloth. Good on you, mate, an' may you stay one step ahead of ever'body what wants to knock your pins from beneath you."

"Good fortune to you as well." Paul clinked his glass against Gabriel's bottle, then drank.

Watching the two, Matt realized again that he never understood the dynamic his two friends had. Get either one of them apart from the other, and they both swore they hated the other. But when they were together, they seemed to understand each other implicitly.

While carousing through London after dark during one of his father's lengthy absences three years ago, Matt had struck up a friendship with Gabriel. Of course, it hadn't started out that way. In the beginning Matt had been another one of Gabriel's marks, the victim of one of his many scams.

The friendship had begun when Matt tracked Gabriel down and gave him a thrashing. Or attempted to. Neither of them could say who had gotten the better of the other that night.

Besides the scams, picking pockets, and warehouse theft, Gabriel hustled every other job he could find that most people would find disreputable or offensive. For one, he hired youngsters to catch rats, then sold them to sporting men to wager on in illegal blood sports.

And he wasn't above picking up the occasional corpse and selling it to the medical schools through the back door. The schools never asked where he got the bodies, as long as they didn't look freshly murdered.

Gabriel resumed his watch over the rest of the pub. Too cheap to provide proper lanterns, the pub owner set out only candles to light tables. Gabriel kept the candle shoved away so that he could lean back and disappear into the shadows.

"So what was it brought you 'ere near straightaway after your father's death?" Gabriel asked.

"I have a job for you," Matt said. "If you're interested."

"What's the job?" Gabriel asked.

"I want you to follow a man for me. Find out where he goes. Who he sees."

"Sounds easy enough. Unless 'e doesn't do 'is business in a part of town where I fit in, or where I can hire eyes to watch for me. Who's the man?"

"Inspector George Donovan."

A look of distaste wrinkled Gabriel's mouth and forehead. "The Scotland Yard bull?"

"Yes."

"What's the matter?" Paul answered. "Does the assignment sound too risky?"

"Oh," Gabriel replied unhappily, "there's risk involved, all right. Anytime you start messin' with Old Bill—and by that, Master Chadwick-Standish, I'm referrin' to the constabulary what polices London proper—you run a powerful lot of risk. Them bobbies sticks together, they does. You mess with one of them, you might as well have whacked a hornet's nest because they's all gonna come after you. Ain't nuffink to do then but start runnin' for your life." He sipped from the bottle. "An' George Donovan? 'E was a thievin' man's worst nightmare even before 'e went an' got 'isself promoted to inspector."

"What do you mean?" Matt asked.

"I means 'e 'ad 'is 'and in the till, guv." Gabriel leaned closer and lowered his voice. "You see, Donovan was one of them sly coppers. 'E'd bust a few 'eads of thieves, cut them a deal now an' again by lettin' 'em go an' takin' the goods what they risked their necks to steal, an' then 'e'd start settin' them up for other jobs. For a share in the take."

"Donovan cased jobs for thieves?" Matt asked.

"Yes. Ferreted 'em out, put together a crew, an' made sure ever'thin' went smooth."

"Have you ever done business with Donovan?" Paul asked.

Gabriel narrowed his eyes. "What are you askin'? Ain't gonna get all 'igh an' mighty on me if'n I did, are you?"

"No," Paul replied. "But if you're known to Donovan, he might see you. Things could get very dangerous for you."

A sly grin warped Gabriel's mouth. "Are you worried about ol' Gabriel then, guv?"

"If things get dangerous for you, they get dangerous for Matt. I don't want to see that happen."

Gabriel was quiet for a time. "There's somethin' you ain't tellin' me. Why would Donovan start thinkin' 'e might be followed?"

"Because," Matt said, taking a deep breath, "I think Donovan is working for the men who killed my father."

"I 'eard your father's death was an accident."

"It wasn't."

"Then why ain't you beatin' down the door to Scotland Yard an' tellin' them blokes?"

"Because," Matt said, "this thing is more complicated than you would imagine. And I don't have any tangible proof about my father's murder."

Gabriel turned his hands up. "Convince me."

As Matt talked about Scanlon and Creighdor and much of what had happened the evening before, Gabriel took a sixpence coin from his pocket and began flipping it across the knuckles of his right hand with dexterity a stage magician would envy. He never once interrupted till Matt finished describing the encounter with Donovan.

"Goaded you into a fight is what 'e done," Gabriel said. "Made you look bad in front of them newsies."

Matt's face burned. "That wasn't immediately apparent to me then."

"Wasn't supposed to be. 'E's a clever one, that Donovan is."

"Which means you'll have to be twice as clever when you follow him," Paul pointed out.

"You don't know 'ow come 'im to just show up at yer door?" Gabriel asked Paul.

"No. Of course, if a person were looking for Matt, one of the first places he or she would look is my parents' house. It's a simple process of elimination for anyone who knows us."

"True," Gabriel said, "but there 'ad to be somebody what give Donovan that list to begin with. An' if Donovan come out there 'isself instead of some other policeman, why ye can bet it was 'im the list was give to. Not Scotland Yard."

"But who could give Donovan such a list?" Paul asked.

"Exactly." Gabriel pointed at Paul. "Mayhap the two of you can cipher that one out. In the meantime, I'll keep an eye on your Inspector Donovan. As for Scanlon an' Creighdor, I'll keep me eyes an' ears open for what I can see an' 'ear about them too."

"It could be dangerous," Matt reminded.

Gabriel waved the possibility away. "Why, it'll keep me sharp is all. Don't like gettin' fat an' lazy." He scratched his chin. "What about yer father's book? The one you mentioned 'e showed you in the flat?"

"It was burned in the fire," Matt said.

Nodding, Gabriel said, "I figured as much since you didn't mention it. But I was talkin' about the *other* book."

Mystified, Matt leaned in. "What other book?"

"There's gotta be another book," Gabriel insisted. He looked surprised, as if his line of thinking was something Matt and Paul should have already thought about. "A man as careful as your father, why 'e'd keep two books about 'is business an' 'is affairs. Copies of each other, they'd be. Didn't 'e do that?"

Matt shook his head. "I don't know."

Gabriel looked at Paul. "You do investments. Don't you keep two books?"

Paul frowned. "Yes."

"See?" Gabriel switched his attention back to Matt. "Ever'body I know what works with money or other valuables, why, they keeps two books. Sometimes more, depending on how truthful they's bein' with their taxes. But somethin' like this?" He nodded. "Your father, 'e would keep two books. One for 'is own use an' another for someone else to find in case somethin' 'appened to 'im. 'E wouldn't 'ave wanted 'is crusade to die with 'im. 'E'd 'ave wanted people to know about Creighdor, 'e would." He looked at Matt. "An' I'd expect 'e'd put the other book somewheres you could find it."

Matt swapped looks with Paul.

"Sounds perfectly logical," Paul said. "I should have thought about that myself."

"It's all right, guv," Gabriel said condescendingly. "You'd prolly 'ave gotten back round to 'er in another day or three."

"Then why didn't Father mention another book last night?" Matt asked.

"You said yourself that things 'appened quick-like last night," Gabriel said. "Mayhap 'e intended to. I find it interesting that Creighdor didn't try to 'ave your father killed before last night."

"Maybe he did," Matt said. Guilt over all the things his father had been subjected to rose within him.

"Your father," Gabriel said, "kept a lot of things to 'isself. 'E 'ad to in order to sneak up on Creighdor as 'e did."

"So why did Creighdor hesitate to kill him till now?"

"Mayhap it's the threat of the books."

"Why take the risk now?"

"Because," Paul said, "your father showed you the book."

"Lettin' the cat out of the bag, 'e was," Gabriel added.

"How many others did my father tell?"

"How many people would have listened?" Paul looked immediately embarrassed. "I meant no disrespect, Matt."

Matt nodded.

"You were the first yer father showed, Matt," Gabriel said. "I'd stake me life on it, I would. You were 'is son. 'Is only child. Your father, 'e would show no one else before you. That's the kind of man I 'eard 'im to be."

"But how did Creighdor know Father had shown me the book?" Matt asked.

"The gargoyle?" Gabriel suggested.

Paul said, "There's no other answer."

"There was no time for the gargoyle to report to Creighdor," Matt objected. "Father had only then shown the book to me."

"Some means of communication had to exist," Paul said. "A signal, perhaps."

Gabriel nodded. "Or the gargoyle 'ad its orders."

"Wouldn't Creighdor know there might be another copy of the book?"

"I think that's why 'e let you run," Gabriel said.

"I escaped."

"They didn't try 'ard enough to get you," Gabriel said.

Matt didn't want to believe that. Thinking that way made him feel exposed and vulnerable.

"Doesn't mean they would 'ave caught you," Gabriel said, as if guessing Matt's thoughts. "Just means they didn't try because they wanted you runnin' loose."

"To find the other book?" Matt asked. "If it even exists?"

"It exists," Paul said. "I believe Gabriel deduced that correctly."

"The book," Gabriel said, "poses a threat to Creighdor somehow. Or maybe there's somethin' in it 'e wanted. There was a lot yer father didn't get to tell you."

"No one wanted to believe my father."

"Mayhap," Gabriel said, "somethin's about to 'appen what will change all that."

The threat of Gabriel's words lay naked and ugly between them.

"This shipment what come in," Gabriel said, "must be mighty important."

Matt thought about that. "But the second book—"

"Could be the most important," Paul said. "I would suggest we invest our energies in that direction."

Matt looked at his friends. "If I lead Creighdor and his men to the second book, I'll be playing right into their hands."

"Not searching for the book isn't the answer," Paul said. "I would bet that your father left it in a place only you can find."

"An' if you get the book," Gabriel put in, "it could be the most dangerous weapon you can put yer 'ands on if you want to strike back at Creighdor."

Matt took his pocket watch out of his vest and flipped it open to reveal the time. "If we hurry, we can catch a train out to the estate home."

"Do you think your father would leave the second book there?" Paul asked. "Seems a trifle unprotected and overly expected if he thought he had to hide it from his enemies."

"Do you have someplace else in mind we could look?" Matt countered.

After a brief hesitation, Paul said, "No."

"Then we try there first." Matt plucked his hat up from the table. "Gabriel?"

"I'll find Donovan," Gabriel promised. "Whatever 'e's up to, you'll soon know it. An' I'll come to you straightaway." He leaned back into the shadows. "But if you two are goin' out to the country, you be careful. After this mornin' with Inspector Donovan, mayhap Creighdor an' this Scanlon knows you might be a tad bit more dangerous than they bargained on. Step lively as you go."

Matt and Paul caught the train to Cambridge with only minutes to spare. The metropolitan train depot at London Bridge's Briarean station was an overgrown tangle of tracks and engines laid side by side. The large passenger waiting areas beneath the canopied roofs were filled with people, the cacophony of thunder created by the pulling engines, and the eye-stinging cinders and ash from the flaming wood boxes as the engineering teams stoked them to capacity.

Despite the lateness of their arrival, they had no problem securing first-class passage. As the conductor rang his bell and bawled the final boarding call, they stepped up into the first-class car and found and empty compartment.

When the pulling engine jerked into motion, whipping the cars behind it, Matt saw that his friend was already fast asleep. He stared through the open windows and saw the dark clouds that promised rain to the south.

He took his pocket watch out and checked the time. It was three minutes after twelve. The trip would take only an hour and ten minutes. He studied his mother's picture inside the watch cover for a time, then closed and put it away.

I will find the answers, Father. I swear that to you.

"Wake up. We're here." Matt shook Paul beside him as the train slowed and pulled into the tiny station of Foxbarrow.

Rain fell from the dark heavens, collecting in puddles across the muddy ground. Foxbarrow was a quaint village that existed only as a nod to the gentry who kept sprawling ancestral homes in the surrounding area.

A weather-beaten wooden platform shoehorned into a small, now-abandoned store awaited new arrivals. Holes in the thatched awning allowed the rain to pour through.

"Well," Paul grumped, ducking the small torrents of rain water that sluiced through the holes, "this is certainly a bit more of a hovel than I remembered."

Matt did his best to avoid mud holes as they made their way from the platform to the small stable a short distance from the abandoned store.

Inside, Matt walked over to the stable hand. Mortimer Havers had seven sons, and they all looked like their father, stout and blocky with blunt features and fair hair.

"Geoffrey, isn't it?" Matt asked the young man about his age.

The stable hand took tackle from the wall and glanced at Matt. "Yes sir, Master Matthew. May I be of service to you, sir?"

"I'll need two horses," Matt answered. "Sure-footed mounts with some spirit to them. Not one of the lagabouts used to pull the carriages."

A few minutes later Geoffrey returned, leading two horses. Rain glistened in the dark coats of both animals. They snorted and stamped their hooves in displeasure.

Matt seized the lead horse by its harness and led the animal to one of the paddocks. "Does your father still keep that old army Martini-Henry rifle he uses to control pests?"

"Yes sir, he does."

"Would it be possible to borrow that? I'll gladly pay for the rent of it."

Geoffrey looked at Matt for a long moment, then decided not to ask any questions. "Let me get it for you."

Rain continued to fall. It felt like cool feathers dusting Matt's face. The chugging train engine sounded in the distance, and the heavy gray-black pall of its dragon's breath hung in the air, grudgingly dissipating in the precipitation. The horses' hooves smacked wetly against the soft ground.

Matt led the way along the thin trail that ran to Lord Brockton's estate. *My estate*, he couldn't help thinking, and the thought felt strange snaking through his mind.

In years past, the road to the estate had been more than just a path. But that had been when Lady Brockton had entertained guests at parties despite her husband's halfhearted protests. Roger Hunter hadn't liked all the days of preparation for the events, but Matt remembered his father had always enjoyed the company.

Now only a few ruts remained of the road, and most were filled with rocks and weeds. Even small saplings had sprouted in the open area to close off entrance to the estate.

How long will it be, Matt wondered, *before it looks like no one ever came this way?*

Topping the final ridge, Matt reined in his horse and gazed down at the estate.

Besides the main house, three guest cottages were laid out inside the wall. Beyond them was a large carriage house and stable to hold the horses. Orchards and gardens separated all of the buildings, providing a modicum of privacy, but a common area where an outside pit could be fired up and tables set out for parties and banquets united the four dwelling places.

Matt's eye wandered back behind the main house, to the small plot of land that held the crypts of the family's dead. Weeds and creepers festooned the arched crypts and alabaster pillars, looking like abandoned spider webbing draped over the mausoleums.

The crypts would have to be cleaned, Matt decided. Right now they were not fit for a burial. He doubted many would come to his father's funeral, but he wouldn't have the funeral there in the state of disrepair that existed.

He urged the horse onward again, soaked to the skin by the rain that continued to spit and sail through the leaden sky.

Chapter 6

Lord Brockton."

Matt was surprised by Finsterwald's greeting. For as long as he could remember, Herbert Finsterwald had been the estate's major-domo. He had doted on Matt's mother, treating her like the daughter he had never had, and his friendship with Roger Hunter was much closer than master and servant.

Atop his horse, Matt stared down at the butler.

Herbert Finsterwald was an ex-military man with whom Lord Brockton had served in the Crimean War. Both men told stories of how the other had saved his life and they'd become friends forever after as a result.

He wore black and the color suited him well, lending him authority and polish. His gray hair, only a fringe at the back and at the sides, was carefully combed. He was smooth-shaven and his cheeks gleamed.

"You've heard then?" Matt asked, his voice thick with sudden emotion.

"Yes. Only just. One of the Havers boys came by to tell us the news. He'd talked with someone who arrived on the seven o'clock train. I'd hoped and prayed that it wasn't true, but I see you and Master Paul here before me now and I know it must be."

"It is," Matt said.

Finsterwald's hazel eyes misted and his lips quivered. "I was told your father was lost in a terrible accident."

Matt shook his head. "It was no accident, Herbert. My father fell in battle."

"Battle?"

"Yes. Come into the house. There's a lot we must talk about."

"Let me tend to your horses, Lord Brockton. Master Paul, it is good to see you again." Finsterwald started from the porch.

"It is good to see you again, Mr. Finsterwald," Paul replied.

Matt looked at the old man and saw that the years and his father's madness had taken much from Finsterwald as well. None of them, it appeared, had been left unmarked. "We will tend to the horses. If you can see your way clear, I'd like a pot of tea made ready. And biscuits if you can find them. Paul and I have made our journey here on empty stomachs."

"And through this blasted rain," Paul put in. "It's enough to leave a body chilled to the bone."

"I'll see to it at once."

"Thank you." Matt guided his horse to the dilapidated stable in back of the main house. He stripped off the wet saddle and put it aside to dry, then fed and watered the horse.

"Always take care of the animals first," Paul said, smiling. "I remember your father constantly telling us that when we came back from riding."

Matt nodded, and took a little pride in the fact that his father had left such an impression on Paul. "It's a good rule. Father always said you could tell the kind of man you were dealing with by the way he cared for his animals and his tools."

Shouldering the cartridge bag containing the extra rounds for the rifle, Matt slipped the Martini-Henry from the saddle scabbard and carried the weapon across his shoulder.

"Do you think the rifle is necessary inside the house?" Paul asked.

"I sincerely hope not," Matt answered.

Matt told the story of his father's death in the small breakfast nook off the formal dining room. Herbert had given Matt lessons in music—the cello and the violin—and history, primarily martial history, in that same room.

"Well," Finsterwald said when Matt had finished the account, "there is a small comfort in that your father was murdered by his enemies. You'll forgive me, Lord Brockton, but even I had begun to have doubts about your father's sanity over the years. I should have taken better care of him."

"You did take care of him," Matt said softly. "If you hadn't been here, I don't think he would have lasted as long as he did. Nor would I."

"I watched you both slip away there at the end," Finsterwald said. "Your father off to chase what I thought were his brokenhearted imaginings, and you to find a better life than the one you had here. I felt helpless to deal with either event."

"Well," Matt said in a thick voice, "I'm back and things are going to be different. We've a mission, Herbert. I intend to bring to justice the men who murdered my parents."

"Yes, my lord." Finsterwald's voice hardened. "But what you're talking about doing—" He paused. "It's going to be very dangerous."

"It's going to be dangerous for Creighdor, Scanlon, and their lackeys as well."

"You have your father's smile," Finsterwald said, "when you talk like that. He always wore that fierce smile when the action was at its worst in the Crimea. I'd never noticed that on you before."

Feeling a little embarrassed, Matt nodded.

"Perhaps it's because I've never been where I am today before." He cleared his throat. "I need to ask you to do something."

"Anything, my lord. Just as I did for your father. You know that."

Matt had to clear his throat twice more before he could force the words out. "I need you to go into London. To arrange for my father's burial. I've—I've never done anything like that before. The body will need to be brought home. I wouldn't know who to talk to."

"Of course, my lord. I'll gladly take care of it."

"The grounds will have to be cleaned up before the funeral takes place. Speak with Geoffrey Havers down at the Foxbarrow station and see if he can put the word out for labor. I know there are families in the area that can use the money."

"Yes, my lord. When should I get started?"

"The sooner the better, Herbert."

"Then, if you'll excuse me, I'll be on my way." Finsterwald stood and inclined his head.

"There is one other thing," Matt said. "Do you know where my father kept his books? Personal journals he wanted kept hidden?"

"It's not here, Matt." In disgust, Paul flopped onto the divan at the foot of the big four-poster bed. A cloud of dust swelled up around him. Roger Hunter had forbidden the maids to clean the bedroom, and even Finsterwald's efforts had been rebuffed more than once.

Matt sat at his father's rolltop desk and peered over the mountains of letters, journals, and pamphlets he and Paul had searched through during the last few hours. They'd found no mention of Creighdor or Scanlon in any of them. A search of the study and the library had produced the same results.

Matt felt that was true. "Then where else do we look? The flat in Piccadilly was destroyed. I doubt anything in it survived."

"One book was there," Paul said. "Your father wouldn't have kept the second one there as well." He rubbed the silver falcon on his walking stick. "What we need to produce is a chain of logic that will offer us a clue as to what your father was thinking."

"Nothing about this is logical. My father, although he was correct about so many things, might not have been logical." Matt felt the anger growing inside him and could scarcely contain it. "What secrets could Creighdor possibly have that would make my father a danger to him?"

Paul spoke quietly. "Your father wasn't the danger. Not at first."

Cold realization spread through Matt.

"Creighdor and his people didn't murder your father first, Matt."

"They murdered my *mother*."

"Yes." Paul nodded. "She must have somehow

become a threat first. So they killed her. We have to surmise that if your father had known whatever she found out, they would have killed him as well. They hadn't counted on his pursuing them with single-minded purpose the way he has these past seven years. Creighdor and Scanlon made a resourceful enemy and did not know it."

"They have made another," Matt stated.

"I know," Paul said solemnly. "However, your mother's connection can't be explored with what we know. For now, we need to fathom your father's thinking."

Again anger surged within Matt. "My mother did nothing wrong, Paul."

Paul stayed still and spoke very quietly after a deliberate pause. "I didn't say she did, Matt. That was not an accusation. Merely an acknowledgment of two separate incidents. I am only trying to think all of this through."

Matt pushed up from his father's chair and paced the room. "I know. I'm sorry. It's just that this—*all* of this—is almost more than I can bear."

"I know of no one else who could face this as well as you have so far," Paul told him. "I know I could not."

Matt went to the window and stared out. In the distance, through the hard rainfall of the storm, he barely made out the greenhouse his mother had spent so many winters and springs in. The eastern sky was starting to turn dark with the approaching night, but the grounds outside were visible.

"Your father told you about the book that night," Paul went on. "Then there has to be another place. A place that your father was certain only you and he knew about."

Memory surged within Matt, and he felt foolish he hadn't thought of it before. He turned back to the window. "Mother's greenhouse."

"What?"

"A secret place my father *may* have known about." Frenzied now, Matt picked up the Martini-Henry rifle from where he had left it by his father's desk, then looped the bag holding spare cartridges for the rifle over his shoulder. "Follow me."

He plunged through the house, feeling a fever burn through him, knowing he was right. He *had* to be right. He took the stairs down to the first floor, then darted out the back through the kitchen.

A short trail led from the kitchen to the greenhouse under the sheltering boughs of trees filled with whispering leaves. In only a short time night would be upon them and would rob them of the light that could help them in their search.

The greenhouse was an elaborate structure made of wrought iron and glass. Seeing some of the panes cracked and others broken out distressed Matt.

Long tables filled the available space inside the greenhouse. When his mother was alive, flowers, shrubs, and bushes had flourished even in the dead of winter due to the heating system his father had designed in the structure.

Now those tables bowed under the weight of rows of pots containing dead things. The greenhouse had become as much a mausoleum as the crypt was.

Matt halted at the small well in the center of the greenhouse. The builders had tapped into an underground stream and built the artesian well above it. The water level was always maintained.

"What are we doing here?" Paul asked as he came to a stop behind Matt. He carried both their coats.

"You talked about a secret place." Matt leaned the rifle beside the well and knelt. He counted stones set into mortar in the side of the well. "I had all but forgotten this one."

Curious, Paul knelt beside him but took the time to pull on his coat against the chill that filled the greenhouse.

"My mother loved this place," Matt said as he explored the well's side with his fingertips. "She worked out here whenever she could. Brought her friends here."

"I remember. I was always astounded with the amount and varieties of flowers she grew here."

"But there was something you didn't know. Something only my mother and I knew." Matt found the stone he was searching for, annoyed that he hadn't known it immediately. He locked his fingertips around the edges of the stone and pulled.

Grating a little, the stone slid free of the loose mortar. A dark hollow lay revealed.

"Mother found this loose stone," Matt explained as he lay it aside. "Instead of having it repaired, she chose to leave it and even worked the stone so that a hiding place was made. It was our secret. She left trinkets in here for me, and I left little presents for her. Nothing much, really, but we enjoyed having our secret. Much the same, I suppose, as whoever designed the house with its secret passageways. My father found out about those, and there's every possibility that he found out about this one, too."

Reaching inside the hollow space, Matt felt a cloth bag. Paper crumpled inside as he closed his hand on it.

The bag was oilskin, designed to keep against the elements. It was rough, had been treated badly, but remained serviceable.

It was also like none of the gaily wrapped packages his mother had left for him.

Matt loosened the bag's drawstrings and dumped the contents into his palm. A key and a small, folded note fell out.

The key was old and ornate, gone green with

age and shaped like the body of a lion. The key's teeth were formed in the lion's snarling mouth.

"Do you know what the key is to?" Paul asked.

"No." Matt fisted the key, then tucked it into his shirt pocket as he turned his attention to the folded slip of paper. As he opened it, he recognized his father's handwriting at once.

Matt—

If you're reading this it probably means something terrible has happened and I am gone from you without a true explanation. I am dreadfully sorry for that. I'd never intended to leave you, or that our lives should become so strained.

I know you haven't understood everything that I have done of late. Hopefully by this time you'll have some inkling of all that has transpired.

Although that will mean your life is undoubtedly in danger.

Please know that I never stopped loving you. I just could not let your mother's death go unavenged. God forbid I should let that happen.

I love you. I hope you have never had true cause to doubt that, my boy.

Matt's eyes stung and tears rolled down his

cheeks as he read his father's words.

> *This key may be all I have left at this point. And the knowledge that it reveals to you may be all you have to save yourself.*
>
> *I can't tell you any more for fear this key and this message will fall into the treacherous hands of my enemies.*
>
> *Remember what I always said about secrets, my boy. I found out about you and your mother's secret. Remember what I said.*
>
> *Let your heart guide your actions, Matthew. It may be that you will have to flee for your life, and I would not blame you. But my enemies—and yours!—are a threat to our family; they are a definite danger to our dear country.*
>
> *Your mother, had she lived to see me undertake this battle, would have understood. She was a most elegant and unique woman, Matthew, and I miss her sorely. I know that you do as well. Hopefully she will forgive whatever errors I have made that have left you alone and unguarded in this moment.*

At this point the ink was smeared. Though it was now dry, Matt could see where water had blurred the lines.

> *I can't go on, my boy. Even writing this, despite the fact that I know it has to be done,*

breaks my heart.
I love you.
Humbly,
Your Father
Roger Hunter, Lord Brockton

Matt's hand trembled as he held the note. He handed the paper to Paul, who quickly read the words.

"So your father knew about this hiding place?" Paul asked.

"I didn't think so, but you see the evidence to the contrary." Matt wiped the last tears from his face. He pushed his pain and uncertainty away, but the frustration remained.

"What was it he told you about secrets?"

"He used to say the only way two men could keep a secret was if one of them were dead. It was partly a joke, but I knew he was serious too. My father kept his own counsel about a number of things." *And now my father is dead and I can't learn his secrets.*

"The key means something." Paul put his hand on Matt's shoulder. "We'll figure it out. I promise you. We're further now than we were. The rest of it will come. You just have to maintain faith."

"I know." Matt stood and reached for the rifle. Movement on the other side of the glass wall caught his attention.

A man moving slowly and deliberately

through the ruin of the orchard looked like a shadow through the condensation lining the glass. He carried a rifle in his hands as he closed in on the back of the main house.

Chapter 7

Matt grabbed Paul's coat lapels and yanked him to the ground.

"Down!" he hissed.

Paul didn't struggle.

Matt pointed at the man crossing through the overgrown orchard, only then noticing another man on the other side of the greenhouse.

"I see them," Paul whispered.

Matt cursed his own stupidity at not taking other weapons from his father's collection inside the house.

"Thieves, do you think?" Paul asked.

"Do you?"

Paul's answer was immediate. "Not for a moment." He looked around. "We're in a terrific spot of trouble."

Staying low to the ground, Matt crawled toward the greenhouse's back door. "This way."

Paul followed, dragging Matt's coat with him.

Reaching the door, Matt rose to a squatting

position. He looked at the front of the greenhouse and watched as the two men, now joined by a third, gathered close by.

Matt could just barely hear the men. Their voices were low but audible.

"Two of them, then?" one man asked.

"Aye," one of the others said. "That was the main servant we saw at the station in Foxbarrow. Lord Brockton kept this here house shut up while he was livin' in London. Only had other servants here when he was stayin'. He hasn't stayed in a long time."

"Has these two got any guns?"

"Only if they picked up somethin' inside," the third man said. "Scanlon, he says they're young 'uns. Hardly more'n whelps. Shouldn't be no real bother. Says he wants 'em alive."

"Might be we can't do that," the first man said.

"Wouldn't want to be the one what pulls the trigger if it comes to that," the third man said. "Scanlon's got a powerful anger, he has."

Paul handed Matt his coat. "Put this on," he whispered.

As the three men walked toward the rear of the main house, Matt started to shake his head.

"We're going to have to run for it," Paul said. "That's the only real chance we have. If they've got men round to the back of the house, you can be certain they have them in front as well. Won't do for you to perish from sickness if we manage to dodge a bullet."

Acknowledging the wisdom of his friend's words, Matt pulled on the coat. He waited, hand on the greenhouse doorknob, until one of the men tried the main house's back door and walked inside.

Matt opened the greenhouse door and stepped outside quickly, pushing the door ahead of him. The door stopped movingly suddenly, causing him to slam into it.

"Well 'ello," a bearded man with a Cockney accent and a bowler hat announced. He stood on the other side of the door, one huge foot braced against it. He lifted a revolver in one hand and pointed it at Matt's head.

Matt was unable to squeeze through the opening and knew trying to escape through the front of the greenhouse was out of the question.

"What say you two gents come along without no fuss?" the big man suggested. "Ain't no sense in you bein' 'urt if'n you don't 'ave to be." His grin got broader. "An' right now, I ain't bein' paid to 'urt you."

Matt dropped and slammed his shoulder into the door, driving himself forward and knocking the man backward. The revolver went off with a sharp report that was deafening, but thankfully the bullet didn't blast through his skull and kill him on the spot.

Plunging through the door, Matt brought the

rifle barrel round and caught the man's wrist as he tried to aim the pistol again. Bone broke and the pistol flew free. The man screamed in pain and rage, but Matt swung the rifle like a wicket and clubbed the side of his head, knocking him out.

"Come on!" Matt cried urgently. He glanced back over his shoulder at the rear of the main house.

The three men at the back door had dived for cover at the sound of the shot. Their rifle barrels poked out.

"There they are!" someone shouted.

"The stables," Paul said.

"Go," Matt said. "I'm right behind you." He stooped to recover the man's dropped pistol and put it into his coat pocket.

Paul ran for the stable, taking advantage of every bit of cover available. Shots splintered branches in his wake.

"That redheaded 'un we don't need, you blokes," one of the men shouted from behind a rain barrel. "It's the one with dark hair that Scanlon really wants to talk to. Cut that 'un down an' let's lessen our troubles."

Dropping to one knee in a crouched position, Matt brought the heavy rifle to his shoulder and took aim at the speaker. Never in his life had he fired at a man, but there was only the briefest hesitation in him now as shots kicked at Paul's heels.

Matt centered the rifle's open sights over the man's head, then shifted ever so slightly to the left and slid his finger over the trigger. He pulled smoothly, then rode out the weapon's massive recoil.

The man jumped backward and ducked behind cover.

The other two men rapidly dug more deeply into the shelters they'd chosen. Evidently they weren't quite as brave against targets that shot back.

"He's got a rifle!" someone yelled.

Matt took a moment to work the rifle's action and feed a new cartridge into the breech. He didn't let the fear that he was about to be shot lessen his concentration.

He got up and ran, plunging through the trees, brush, and weeds that had grown up inside the estate. His breath came in ragged gasps, but it was more from his emotions running rampant than the physical exertion.

When he reached the stable, the three men had recovered their nerve and fired at him. Bullets whacked into the sides of the building, splintering wood and spooking the horses.

Paul already had a bridle slung over the head of his mount.

"No time for saddles," he said, throwing Matt the other bridle.

Matt caught the bridle and slung the rifle over his shoulder so the barrel pointed down. His wet clothes pulled at him. He caught his horse's harness after three failed attempts, then pulled the bridle into place.

Paul leaped up onto his own horse and barely controlled the fear-maddened animal as it jumped and wheeled. He held onto his walking stick with difficulty.

Climbing up the side of the stall once he had the bridle in place, Matt opened the gate and vaulted onto the horse's back. The rifle thumped against him as the horse bucked and reared and finally gave in.

"Round back," Matt called. "We'll go up into the hills. There's cover there we can use."

"Lead the way," Paul responded.

Pulling the horse's head toward the rear of the barn where a low fence blocked passage to an open field, Matt dug his feet into the animal's flanks and yelled, "He-yaahhh!"

The horse drummed its hooves against the straw-covered ground. Matt heard Paul curse behind him, but he also heard the other horse charging after him. The fence was low enough that it wouldn't take a steeplechaser to get over. The horse halted a few feet short of the fence, gathered itself, then leaped with inches to spare. But, landing on the other side on the muddy ground the animal's hooves sliced through the earth like a surgeon's scalpel and it lost its footing.

As the horse went down on its rump, Matt

pushed himself from the animal's back. Running, his instinct honed by years of riding with and without saddles, he kept pace with the horse till it once more got its footing and plunged forward. As surefooted as a circus acrobat, Matt caught the horse's mane and heaved himself onto its back once more.

Bullets whipped through the trees overhead. Branches broken by shots tumbled down over him and he knocked others aside with his free arm. He stayed low over the horse, partly to avoid the tree limbs and partly to take cover from the men shooting.

Glancing back, Matt saw that Paul had adopted a similar riding style.

Back at the main house, six other men joined the first three attackers. All of them were armed. They took up pursuit at once, still occasionally firing shots. One of the men split off and came back leading horses that had been tethered behind one of the guesthouses.

Matt saw the open rear gate at the back of the grounds. The muddy tracks cutting through the overgrown road gave away their attackers' means of entrance.

Rain pelted Matt's face, causing him to squint to see more clearly.

Two men on horseback guarded the gate. They had rifles.

Reaching into his coat pocket, Matt pulled out the revolver and thumbed back the hammer.

He fired with the pistol extended above the horse's ears, aiming his first two shots at the guards' horses' feet. The pistol unfamiliar bucked ferociously against Matt's hand as rain slapped his face. Thankfully, the horse didn't spook out from under him at the crack of each shot. But then, these horses were trained for hunting and so were accustomed to the crash of weapon fire.

The first round dug into the ground in front of the man, clawing out a fist-sized hole. The horses began to rear out from under the men. Matt heard a heavy rifle bullet cut the air beside his ear and knew that the miss had been a near thing.

The men, unable to control their mounts, abandoned their posts.

Matt and Paul rode through the gate. Matt looked behind and saw that the group at the house had mounted up and were in pursuit.

The hill behind the family estate was long and tall. Trees dotted the landscape.

At the top of the rise, Matt pulled his mount to a stop and slid off. He wrapped the bridle reins round a branch of the nearest tree, then took up his rifle and walked back to the ridge.

Paul wheeled his own mount around and rode back. "What are you doing?"

"We can't escape them."

"Not if you don't ride."

"There are too many of them, Paul." Matt couldn't believe how calm he was. But he seemed to feel his father at his side. "They have to be stopped now."

Paul cursed. "We have a lead."

"Only for a time." Matt stretched out across the ridgeline, brought out the bag of cartridges, and glanced at the six riders coming up the long grade. "They'll come after us. Maybe they would get lucky. I don't want to risk that."

"What are you going to do?"

Matt shoved the rifle ahead of him and sighted on the lead rider. "I'm going to stop them." He took up the trigger slack and squeezed off the round. The Martini-Henry slammed painfully against his shoulder.

The rider's horse spooked and bucked the man off.

By that time, Matt had another round chambered. He took aim as the rest of the riders tried to find cover. He fired twice more, both times hitting close to his targets and driving them to cover across the hillside.

Return fire chewed holes in the ground ahead of Matt and knocked branches from trees. As the men started getting into range, he pulled back and picked different spots, never allowing them to gain an inch.

As he reloaded, Matt saw one of the men remove a small box from inside his jacket. The metal surfaces of the box gleamed and bright green light flashed in the man's hands.

"That looks like some sort of apparatus," Paul

said. He lay on the ridgeline only a short distance away, holding a small pair of field glasses to his eyes.

"What kind of apparatus?" Matt fitted the proffered field glasses to his eyes and peered down the slope.

The man looked different from the others. He'd moved more quickly, more efficiently through the brush. Twice Matt could have sworn he'd had the man in his sights, but the man had moved away at the last second.

The box he held was only a little larger than his fist. It was oblong, with switches and dials.

And it held a glowing green light that was not the result of a flame or a spark.

Where is the power source? Matt knew he was looking at the impossible. The apparatus the man held couldn't work like that; it couldn't make light. Especially not light bright enough to be seen even on a rainy day near sunset.

Even as he realized that, he wondered what the apparatus did. For surely the man had taken the device out for a reason.

A hum sounded overhead just as Paul called out, "Matt!"

Rolling over, Matt saw Paul scrambling to get away from the flying gargoyle that suddenly swooped and crashed through the tree branches and dropped almost on top of him. Paul whipped the cover from his walking stick and bared the blade as he got to his feet.

The gargoyle looked a lot like the one that had attacked the hansom cab Matt had been in only last night. Horns crowned its demonic face. Wings jutted from its back. Its body, Matt knew, was carved of blue-gray stone, but it moved effortlessly, as if it were made of flesh or something far more malleable.

Paul slashed the gargoyle with the sword, but the edge only grated across the stone skin. With catlike quickness the gargoyle seized the sword blade in a huge three-fingered hand. The blade snapped with a metallic ring.

Paul ducked beneath the gargoyle's claws.

Matt guessed that the man with the mysterious box must have somehow called or alerted the gargoyle. He wondered if the destruction of the box would stop the creature, or if it would continue to operate independently.

With Paul's life on the line, however, there was only one choice he could make. He pulled the heavy rifle to his bruised and aching shoulder as he rose.

Seeing what he had in mind, Paul shook his head. "Don't! You might hit—"

Matt knew his friend hadn't seen what the gargoyle was capable of, how it had destroyed the hansom cab and its driver.

"Duck," Matt ordered, settling his sights over the back of the gargoyle's head.

Paul went to ground. The gargoyle raised a foot, preparing to bring it down and slash its prey. But it turned its head too, looking back at Matt with liquid silver eyes. The broad face was set, immobile, with fangs that ran down either side of its thin-lipped mouth. It raised its batlike wings as if preparing to pounce.

Does it think? Matt wondered. *Does it know I'm about to kill it? Does it care?*

Those thoughts blew apart as he squeezed the trigger. The recoil knocked him back and felt like it had surely torn his arm from its socket this time. The rush of black powder smoke obscured the gargoyle for a moment.

Panicked, wondering if the thing had managed to squash Paul like a bug in spite of his quick action, Matt peered through the smoke. His hands moved automatically to reload the rifle.

The gargoyle stood still as a statue. One leg was raised, only inches from Paul's face. The rifle bullet had smashed into the thing's face between the lower lip and chin, taking off the head from that point up. Electrical sparks jumped in the hollow neck cavity, and tiny plumes of smoke threaded up to be swept away by the wind.

"Paul," Matt called.

"I'm all right." Almost paralyzed by the close call as well as the astonishment of what he was looking at, Paul crawled away from the inanimate creature as it stood on one broad, splayed foot that would have been more at home on a frog or a toad.

Matt crossed to his friend and pulled him to his feet.

"What you said about the gargoyles," Paul gasped, unable to tear his eyes from the thing. "It was true, Matt."

"I know." Matt shoved Paul toward his horse.

"That thing was alive."

"Now it's not." Matt walked back to the ridgeline.

The man with the strange apparatus trudged up the hillside.

Mercilessly, Matt stepped into view with the rifle to his shoulder. He put the sights in the center of the man's chest, telling himself that the man had somehow summoned or controlled the gargoyle with the strange box, and that he would have caused Paul Chadwick-Standish's death if he could have.

The man halted and looked up at Matt. His face was handsome and cruel. There was no fear on his features. He smiled, as if daring Matt to pull the trigger.

Matt fired.

The bullet caught the man in the chest and knocked him backward ten feet. He landed on his back and lay still for a moment. The apparatus with the green light was thrown free but continued to blink.

Reloading, Matt took aim at the box and shot it. Pieces flew in a blaze of sparks bright enough to hurt Matt's eyes.

Then the man he'd shot sat up.

"You shot him," Paul stated hoarsely over Matt's shoulder. "I saw you shoot him. You hit him dead center in the chest. I saw his shirt jump."

The man stood and stared at Matt for a moment as he reloaded the rifle. Then, just as Matt pulled the rifle to his shoulder again, the man stepped behind a tree and disappeared.

Matt felt panic set in again, a primitive fear of the unknown. He turned to Paul, who held the reins of his horse. Without a word he slung the rifle over his shoulder and hauled himself onto the horse, put his heels to the horse's flanks, and let the animal have its head. He wanted nothing more than to put distance between Paul and himself and the men hunting them. He hoped they reached London alive, then realized that even there they weren't going to be truly safe.

Chapter 8

"Well, what do you think?" Gabriel asked, looking bright-eyed and eager in the gray dawn of morning.

Matt envied Gabriel his enthusiasm and energy, but at the same time he knew that his friend had been up and about all night. From their previous excursions together, Matt knew Gabriel rarely went to bed before dawn but was always up before noon. He needed little sleep and was driven to keep moving at all times.

Matt and Paul had returned to London from Foxbarrow the previous evening and spent the remainder of that night at Paul's house. Gabriel came round early that morning to collect them, saying he had news.

"I think," Paul said, pulling his coat more tightly around him in the thick, cold air that rolled in from the Thames, "that mornings are absolutely horrible. Especially wet ones. They should be greeted in bed, on the other side of a window, with a hot meal brought to your room."

The city lay choked and oppressed by the damp weather and the dark streamers of smoke chugging from the chimneys of packinghouses and manufacturing plants. Some mornings, between the humidity and the smoke, Londoners swore that the air was thick enough to chew or carve with a knife.

"You're wrong 'bout that," Gabriel said. "Why mornin's an' early evenin's, they's the best for skulkin' an' such."

"That's what we're doing?" Paul asked. "Skulking?"

"Yeah." Gabriel pushed his floppy hat up and back a little. "Ain't it grand?"

"No." Paul's teeth chattered. "The last time I was up this early, I'd been up all night."

"Well, guv, you don't know what you're missin' is all I says." Gabriel leaned back against the alley wall. The young thief looked thoroughly at ease in the Docklands off Hertsemere Road.

"Where is Donovan?" Matt asked.

"Donovan's all right, 'e is," Gabriel promised. "Bloke took 'im a pint from one of 'is fav'rite waterin' holes last night, 'e did. 'Ard stuff, 'twas. Won't be expectin' 'im up for some time. Prolly sleepin' like a babe, 'e is."

"And if he isn't?" Paul asked irritably.

"Then the lad what I got watchin' 'im will pass on the news an' stay wif him till I comes to relief him," Gabriel said. "I ain't one of Little Bo Peep's sheep when it comes to doin' things like this."

A four-story brick warehouse sat sandwiched in between a boat repair shop and another, newer warehouse. The red and yellow banner on the third floor declared the presence of THE FABUKOUS HARN MUSEUM. NEW and PHENOMENAL showed on the banner as well.

"What do you know about the museum?" Matt asked.

"Other than the fact that Donovan is interested in it an' came 'ere three times yesterday while shippin' was goin' on?" Gabriel asked.

"Yes."

"Why, nuffink. Nuffink at all. But I know 'e was interested in what was comin' an' goin', 'e was."

Matt looked at Paul. "Why would a policeman be interested in a museum?"

"I," Paul proclaimed with a smile, "plodded through a classic education and paid attention—which is more than I can say for you, Matt. I see no reason to plod through history still further. My interests lie to the future. That's where profits are to be made. Antiquarians can keep their dust and moldering things."

"Neither a thief nor the son of an English lord have an interest in this museum," Matt mused. "So why does Donovan?"

"Ain't but a little thing, this 'ere museum," Gabriel said. "That's it on the third floor there.

Ain't no bigger'n that. An' 'e's not interested in the museum, mate. 'E's payin' particular attention to deliveries an' purchases."

"You said Donovan cased jobs for thieves," Matt reminded.

"That's right."

"Perhaps this is another job."

Gabriel shook his head. "Ain't nuffink like that in there, guv. Some of them museums, why they keeps gems an' suchlike. But mostly them ones is museums what 'as money. Museums sell off as much as they keep. 'At's what keeps 'em in business more'n anything when they ain't got no gover'ment charter like a lot of 'em don't. This here museum, why it only keeps artifacts. No jewels or baubles. No golden doodads or gembobs or the like."

"Artifacts?"

"Vases. Jugs. Pieces of buildin's an' suchlike. Statues. That sort o' thing."

"Evidently those things are worth something," Matt said. "If people pay to see them."

"Collectibles," Paul said. "Some people who can afford them like to own them. Rather like my father's annoying Swiss clock. There are several connoisseurs of relics among London's high society. Collections of Roman arrowheads and swords found near forts and battles here in England. Now and then a skull or some other disgusting and barbaric trinket that has been passed along through a family."

"Exactly," Gabriel said. "Waste of money if'n you ask me."

"Then why wouldn't a thief be interested in them?" Matt asked.

"Because," Gabriel explained, "them things in a museum, why they ain't worth nuffink till somebody buys 'em an' takes 'em home. Got to let the buyers get attached to the things they buys. Then you snatches 'em an' ransoms 'em back while they're all caterwaulin' over losin' 'em."

"A museum isn't a store. I didn't know they sold things there."

"Everything," Gabriel said, nodding, "is for sale. For a price."

"Why would Donovan watch this museum?" Matt asked.

"Don't know," Gabriel said. "But while I'm watchin' 'im, I'll prolly figure it out soon enough."

"Why don't we have a look at the museum?" Matt suggested.

"Do you think that's wise? Shouldn't we presume to keep a low profile?" Paul asked.

"Creighdor is already looking for us. And we won't be leaving our real names with anyone we talk to." Matt started across the street, moving quickly to avoid a carriage and sidestepping a fresh pile of horse dung. Trouble, he knew, wasn't so easy to avoid.

• • •

"We're a specialty museum," Donald Wentworth stated with a clear Oxford-trained accent.

Matt and Paul followed the man across the hardwood floor of the warehouse containing the museum. The curator was in his late twenties, thin and tall. He had impressive chin whiskers and wild hair. He was also eager to make a sale. Only two other potential buyers roamed the museum.

"We carry a few Roman pieces, of course," Wentworth continued, waving to the rows of display shelves filled with vases, weapons, and armor. "You have to, you see. A few Chinese pieces, some of them rather good. A few Japanese pieces."

Matt took in the shelves and bins of dragons and other fantastical creatures rendered in stone and clay and fine porcelains.

"We even have a few items from the Napoleonic War, and both wars with the Americans. British and Colonial pieces, you know. For variety." He glanced at the two younger men over his pince-nez. "Often, in my dealings, I have found young men fascinated with owning weapons that possess a bloody history. Would you be interested in a sword or a pistol that has seen mortal combat?"

"I wouldn't," Matt answered.

"How bloody is the history of an item like that?" Paul asked.

Wentworth smiled and rubbed his hands as if

sensing a potential client. "You can settle for a sword used in a famous battle. Or perhaps a pistol that has claimed a life or two." He shrugged and raised his eyebrows, placing his hands together behind his back. "Or you can acquire something a bit more . . . extreme."

"How extreme?"

"Only last month I sold a French guillotine to a young gentleman."

"A guillotine?" Paul was trying to look interested, but Matt detected the greenish tinge around his friend's mouth. "Really?"

"Really," Mr. Wentworth assured him, nodding vigorously. "Used prior to the French Revolution in the court of King Louis XVI and Marie Antoinette. Perhaps you have met the young gentleman in your travels. He is something of a gadabout. Arthur Tuttle."

The name meant nothing to Matt.

"I've made Arthur's acquaintance," Paul said. "But I never knew he was interested in French guillotines."

"Oh, I don't think he knew he was interested in one either. Until the day I showed him the one he now owns." Wentworth smiled unctuously. "You might surprise yourself and find something among our selections that you want for your own."

"Quite right," Paul said, playing the *bon vivant* to the hilt. "I await being smitten."

Since Paul was the better at small talk, Matt

let him handle the conversing. Matt wandered along through the stacks and irregular rows of antiquity, trying to see what had obviously interested Donovan. The musky smell of tombs and earthen pits cloyed his nostrils, and it wasn't hard to imagine that many of the objects he saw were fresh turned from the ground in one country or another.

Wentworth apologized for the disorganized state of the museum, saying that they'd only gone into business a few months previously.

Matt walked through piles of Roman and Spanish armor and weapons, each piece connected to some important aspect of history he barely remembered from his classes. Most of them looked like they'd come from the Roman occupation during the construction of Hadrian's Wall.

Other rows held Chinese and Japanese vases as well as statuary of soldiers that were supposed to have been unearthed from the burial grounds of emperors of one dynasty or another. At another time, he might have enjoyed hearing stories about where the pieces came from. But for the moment he was impatient to figure out the mystery of Donovan's visits.

It wasn't until they reached the Egyptian section of the museum that Matt's own interest was piqued. He stared at the coffin-shaped box that occupied a long table and remembered the oblong box that Scanlon's men had unloaded from *Saucy Lass* two nights ago.

Drawn by the coffin, hypnotized by the ornate lid that covered it, Matt stepped away from Paul and Wentworth. What was it that would interest a man like George Donovan, who might be employed by Lucius Creighdor? He ran his hand along the rough stone surface of the box.

A graven image of a man with a strange head-dress adorned the lid. The man held a short crooked staff and a knife in his hands.

"What is this?" Matt asked.

"Ah, did something catch your eye after all?" Wentworth asked.

"Perhaps," Matt replied.

"Are you perhaps an amateur student of Egyptology?" Wentworth circled the table and came to a stop on the other side of the box.

"No."

"How much do you know about Egyptology?"

"Nothing," Matt admitted.

"Egyptology," Paul said, standing next to Matt, "is the study of Egypt. We have Napoleon to thank for the field of instruction, actually."

"Napoleon Bonaparte?" Matt asked, surprised.

"Quite," Paul replied. "In 1798 he sent troops down into Egypt to reconnoiter. Intent on world dominion, as you might recall."

"Yes." Roger Hunter had given Matt numerous examples of battles and military strategy from the war fought between the British and the French on land and on sea. That had been when

Matt was a boy. His mother had acted aghast at those stories because his father had relished telling of the battles and put in bloody details of the carnage and evils of men.

"Those troops brought back things they stole from the tombs of Egyptian pharaohs," Paul said. "Gold and jewels. But also fascinating things that caught Napoleon's attention. He sent more men and equipment down into what has become known as the Valley of the Kings, where so many of the past rulers of Egypt were interred. Napoleon allowed several historians and scientists to accompany those troops on subsequent investigations."

Matt looked at the box again. "This is a coffin?"

"Actually," Wentworth said, "it is a sarcophagus."

"An Egyptian coffin," Paul said. "But not everyone got buried in such an elaborate manner as you see before you. Most deceased Egyptians, the poor and middle class, were wrapped in linen coated with natron salt and placed in much simpler graves. What you see before you is undoubtedly the body of a pharaoh or a pharaoh's wife or child."

"My word, sir, how knowledgable you are," Wentworth enthused solicitously. "This man was an adviser to King Ramses," Wentworth said. "In most cases, your assessment of Egyptian burial practices would be correct in that only royalty were buried in this manner. But occasionally a pharaoh buried someone special to him in the same manner as he was afforded. Perhaps an architect or a scientist."

"You know who this man was?" Matt asked, thinking of the wagon that Josiah Scanlon had arranged to meet the other night.

"Of course." Wentworth smiled. "If we did not know, then this box would contain only the moldering bones of an unfortunate soul who met his maker. As such, the sarcophagus would hardly be a wise investment. Each mummy, you see, simply must tell a story."

"A mummy is inside?" Matt asked.

"Please," Wentworth said, motioning Matt to the foot of the stone box. "Assist me in this and I'll show you."

Matt retreated to the foot of the coffin as Wentworth walked to the head. Together, upon the curator's instruction, they lifted the heavy stone lid and set it aside.

Inside the sarcophagus, a body lay wrapped in gray-white linen bandages. Dust covered the surface of the body and the interior of the sarcophagus.

"Always be careful with the lids," Wentworth admonished, taking out a kerchief and mopping his sweating brow. "The writing on the lids tells the stories of the individuals contained inside. Egyptologists now have a way of decoding the hieroglyphics the Egyptians used to keep records."

"The hieroglyphics," Paul said, "became known to researchers after the translation of the Rosetta Stone in 1822. The Rosetta Stone was also recovered by Napoleon's troops, though it was years before its significance was understood."

Wentworth tapped the side of the sarcophagus in barely restrained excitement. "Meet Pasebakhaenniut, the architect." He frowned. "Although, I distinctly remember him being cleaner the last time I looked in on him."

"Pasebakhaenniut," Matt repeated.

"Yes." Wentworth ran a hand over the detailed mask the mummy wore. "His name, I am told, means 'The star that appears in the city.'"

"Strange name," Paul commented.

"They were Egyptian," the curator insisted. "Many of the things they did seem strange to us by today's standards. The whole process of mummification is outside our realm of true understanding. But we acknowledge the Egyptian people believed in an afterlife and that the body should be cared for until the deceased person's *ka*—what they called the life force and we would term soul—returned to the corpse."

Matt stared down at the mummy, remembering the body in the box delivered by *Saucy Lass*. "How long have you had this mummy?"

Wentworth thought just a moment. "Ten days, I believe. I'd have to check our records for a more accurate answer, of course. But I believe we've only had it for ten days."

Matt let out a tense breath, knowing the mummy in the sarcophagus before him couldn't have been the body in the box he'd seen. There had to be another reason Donovan was watching the museum.

But the mummy was also unique, the only one of its kind in the building.

The weight of the key hanging at the end of the leather strap around his neck drew his attention. If Paul's theories were right and Donovan was in the employ of Creighdor, perhaps the key fit something Roger Hunter had gotten from the museum. It was possible that Donovan knew more about Lord Brockton's business than Matt did.

"Did Roger Hunter, Lord Brockton, ever do business with this museum?" Matt asked.

Paul quickly glanced at him because Matt had broken their plan to avoid notoriety while in the place.

Wentworth paused. "Sir, I'm not in the habit of discussing private business—"

"I am his son. Matthew Hunter."

Wentworth eyed Matt more directly. "I see the resemblance, yes. You favor your father in your features."

"As my mother always insisted."

Heaving a sigh, Wentworth said, "Yes, I knew your father. Terrible bit of business about his death. My condolences, of course."

"Thank you."

"Lord Brockton was a remarkable man," Wentworth said. "Very learned."

"My father was a man of many talents and interests," Matt replied. "What brought him here?"

"As a matter of fact, your father was interested in this very mummy."

"He was?" Matt looked at the mummy with new eyes.

"Yes. Unfortunately, I had to disappoint him."

"Disappoint him how?"

"Lord Brockton wished to purchase the mummy, but that couldn't be managed."

"If it was a matter of money," Paul said quickly, "I'm sure I can rectify that situation."

Wentworth held up a hand. "Money wasn't the issue. As I explained to Lord Brockton, and to Mr. Creighdor before him, this mummy is already sold."

"Did you mean Mr. Lucius Creighdor?" Matt's heart thumped like a blacksmith's hammer.

An uncomfortable look pulled at Wentworth's face. "As I said, I don't like discussing a patron's private affairs."

And if the answer were no, Matt thought, *there would be no need to defend yourself.* "Of course. I withdraw the question."

"You say the mummy is already sold?" Paul asked.

"Yes."

"Yet here it sits."

"The owner is out of the country at the moment," Wentworth said, with a noticeable hesitation. "He's expected back from China over the next two days."

"I could pay you more," Paul offered.

Wentworth licked his lips. "I regret having to disappoint you, sir." He glanced at Matt. "And you as well, Lord Brockton. But I fear I must. I have given my word on the delivery of this mummy. However, I can endeavor to get you another." He looked at them hopefully.

"No," Matt said. "I do want to thank you for your time, though." He offered his hand. There had to be another way to ferret out the mummy's secret and what it meant to Creighdor.

Paul wished the curator good day and they turned to go.

"My lord," Wentworth called.

Matt turned back to face the man.

"I struck a bargain with the man who wants to add this mummy to his private collection," Wentworth said. "He has paid my partner and me half of the amount we agreed on as earnest money. He owes the balance on his arrival. I've heard that there was some problem with his investments in Shanghai, and that was why he left while the mummy was in transit." The curator stopped speaking and turned his hands up.

"So it could be that your patron might not

finish paying you for the mummy," Paul supplied.

"There is that likelihood," Wentworth agreed, "however small."

Smiling confidently, Paul made a show of popping one of his cards out of his sleeve and presenting it to the curator.

Wentworth looked impressed. "Mr. Chadwick-Standish. I have heard of you." He studied Paul further. "You are much younger than I had thought you to be, although I was told you were a young man."

"A young man of means, I hope you were told." Paul flashed his winning smile.

Wentworth smiled and nodded. "Of course." He pocketed the card and patted his pocket. "Whatever the outcome of this transaction, Mr. Chadwick-Standish, I shall report to you. If the buyer permits, I could put you in touch with him."

"I should appreciate that," Paul responded. "I'd also be willing to pay a broker fee for the introduction. You'll find I can be generous, but demanding as well once we have agreed upon a course of action."

"Yes, sir."

"A mummy?" Gabriel raised his eyebrows as he lounged in the gray darkness of the alleyway across from the Fabulous Harn Museum. "Covered in curses an' all that rot? Like to get up the first time I've got me back turned an' go for me throat?" He didn't look happy. "Nothin' was said about me gettin' involved in mummies an' curses an' what-have-you."

"I think the likelihood of curses attached to a mummy or of the dead walking is somewhat on the order of finding a pot of gold at the other end of a rainbow." Paul pulled on his lambskin gloves as he watched the museum.

"You really think that's what ol' Donovan's interested in?" Gabriel glared at the building. "A corpse what's wrapped in all 'em bandages an' magical spells an' the like?"

"My father was interested in that particular mummy," Matt said, his thoughts busy churning over everything he'd discovered. "So was Creighdor. Though the reason for that escapes me."

"Ah." Gabriel smiled, looking over Matt's shoulder. "Then it must be a right popular thing, that mummy of yours."

"Why do you say that?" Paul asked.

"Because ever since you two gents done 'ave walked out of the museum, there's a young 'indu lad been watchin' you."

Chapter 9

A Hindu lad?" Paul started to turn around.

Gabriel grabbed Paul's wrist, preventing him from turning. "Now don't you turn roun' all suddenlike as would a chick what's lost its mum an' give away that I told you about 'im."

Paul turned his attention back to getting a proper fit from his gloves. He offered Gabriel a wan smile. "Touché."

"I'm gonna wait for a proper moment, then I'm gonna point out a ship out on the river, I am. When I does, you take a look at that bloke—careful an' cunnin'like—an' tell me if you've laid your eyes on 'im ever before."

"I very much doubt it," Paul said. "I know few people of the Hindu persuasion."

"An' you too, Matt. Like as not, if neither of you knows 'im, why then 'e's workin' for someone else." Gabriel pointed out toward the Thames. "There you go, lads. Get a look. An' mind you take a look at that two-master out there what's got 'er block-an'-tackle fouled an' causin' a commotion."

Matt turned and saw the cargo ship Gabriel was talking about immediately. Men swarmed the decks and the lines seeking to free the snarled block-and-tackle.

What Matt didn't immediately see was the Hindu man the street thief had caught sight of. Then, before he could ask, he noticed a tall young man lounging near the front of the boat repair shop as if inspecting the river craft stacked upside down on crates and sawhorses.

He looked like he was in his teens, no more than twenty at the most. His dark complexion instantly marked him as a probable foreigner, although a few Chinese and East Indians had established tentative sections within and without London and families were now into their second and third generations. Matt couldn't tell if he was Hindu or not; the young man wore no turban. Black hair framed his face, parted in the middle and hanging down into the round-lensed glasses he wore.

"Certainly no sailor," Paul commented. "Looks more like a shopkeeper's son."

Matt silently agreed with his friend's assessment. The young man wore a good suit and a hat, and he looked out of place standing next to the boat repair shop.

"'E's an 'indu all right," Gabriel said. "Me, I

gots a nose for a man's background. That bloke, he's 'indu. I'll put a pint against you on it."

"Are you certain he was watching us?" Matt asked.

"As sure as I'm standin' here," Gabriel replied. "I first noticed 'im goin' in after the two of you."

"After the two of us?" Paul asked. "And you did nothing to stop him?"

Gabriel nodded and smiled like they were just having a casual conversation. "Thought nothin' of hit at the time. Like prolly 'e was another vis'ter to the museum. But when 'e came out like to near on your footsteps, that's when I marked 'im as somethin' more."

"I'd like to know who he is," Matt said.

"As would I," Gabriel said. "I doesn't like wild cards in a game I'm playin' in."

"I think I'll ask him," Matt said, and he was already in motion.

"Don't," Gabriel warned. "Might not be safe, Matt. A man followin' you roun', why 'e knows there's some dangers. Like as not 'e's come prepared for 'em. Let me—"

But Matt wouldn't be stopped. He felt furious at his helplessness to avenge the murder of his parents and to take on whatever mission his father had left to him.

Lucius Creighdor remained out of reach and Josiah Scanlon was invisible in London's underworld. But the young man across the street was almost within his grasp.

The young man glanced up like a deer sighting a hunter. His eyes rounded to match the lenses of his glasses.

A horse's hooves struck the cobblestones to Matt's right, then a man's voice shouted, "Mind yer step there, ye bleedin' blind oaf!"

From the alley, Paul and Gabriel called out warnings as well.

Only then did Matt realize he'd nearly stepped into the path of a hansom cab. The iron-bound wheels clattered by as the coach cut off sight of the young man for a moment. Matt cursed his inattention, knowing it was a result of too much on his mind and not enough sleep. He walked quickly to the back of the passing coach, close enough to touch the vehicle. The well-dressed man and woman inside drew back from him.

When he got round to the back and his view was clear again, Matt saw that the young man had disappeared. He trotted across the street, followed by Paul and Gabriel, all three of them drawing suspicious stares from businessmen and stevedores, even from the sailors and dock-workers to their right.

Reaching the boats, Matt gazed round in all directions. There was no clue which way the young man had gone, except that Matt was certain his quarry hadn't dived into the river. His temper nearly got the better of him and he held himself under restraint with immense difficulty.

"Did you see which way he went?" Matt demanded.

"No," Paul admitted. "I was more concerned about your welfare at the moment."

"As was I," Gabriel said, gazing around. He threw an arm around Matt's shoulders and pulled him into motion, getting him out of the immediate attention of the people round them. "But not to worry, Matt. We'll know where the blighter was from soon enough."

"What makes you so sure of that?" Paul asked.

"Because," Gabriel said, "when I stakes someone out, I doesn't come by meself. You see, you can get seen by your mark. Or maybe 'e gets skittish an' ups an' moves so quick you're bound to get noticed if you stay at 'im. So I 'ad three of me lads with me this mornin'."

Matt looked around as they walked back along the street away from the museum and the mysterious mummy. "I saw no one."

"'Course not. You weren't supposed to. Why, if'n they stood out like sore thumbs, they'd 'ave not been doin' their jobs. An' I doesn't pays for work what isn't done." Gabriel touched his nose with a forefinger, then pointed to a dirty-faced young boy of eight or nine who stood on the corner near a young girl selling flowers.

The young boy touched his own nose in response.

"See there?" Gabriel asked, grinning. "I didn't

come 'ere to leave you unprotected, Matt. I knows you got enemies like I knows you 'aven't got eyes in the back of yer 'ead."

"Where are the other two lads you said you had?" Paul asked.

"Why, I set them after our 'indu lad. When I figured what 'e was about, I set them lads on 'is trail. As soon as 'e lights, I'll know."

"Bravo, Gabriel," Paul congratulated quietly. "I begin to see why Matt has put so much faith in you."

"It's a faith well earned," Gabriel said. "I doesn't stint when it comes to me friends."

"You'll get word to me about that man's identity?" Matt asked.

"As soon as I know," Gabriel promised. "As soon as I know."

"You'll also keep an eye on Donovan?" Paul asked.

"I'll be 'is bloomin' shadow, I will."

"And you'll keep the mummy under wraps as well? Lucius Creighdor is not a man used to being denied what he wants." Paul smiled a little at his own wit. "Mummy under wraps. I rather liked that one. I shall have to remember that at some later date."

"I'll keep a weather eye peeled for the mummy as well." Gabriel seemed a little disconcerted by that task.

"Splendid," Paul said. "Do remember to have someone watching you. In case the mummy's curse kills you, we should have word of it from someone." He took off walking, hands behind his back holding his walking stick. "Come on, Matt. We should have time to have a bit of breakfast before we meet with your father's barrister this morning."

Gabriel sighed and glanced at Matt. "You're sure there ain't no curse on that mummy?"

"Curses aren't real, Gabriel," Matt said.

"Prolly not to you," Gabriel said. "But I seen me some things that would make a man wonder."

"So have I," Matt said, gazing up at the third-floor museum and thinking about gargoyles. "But whatever there is of interest about that thing, I don't believe it has anything to do with the supernatural."

Then he remembered how Scanlon and the man he'd shot had risen back to their feet, seemingly none the worse for wear. He still had no explanation for the animated gargoyles either, but thinking of the mysterious box the man had used at his family home and the wiring and strange boxes inside the gargoyle was reassuring. None of the magic he'd ever heard of used electricity.

There was a logical answer. There had to be.

"Your father, despite his faults, and God knows every man alive has no few of his own, was a good man, Matt." Medgar Thaylor spoke in a deep, ponderous voice as he sat on the other side of the large inlaid desk.

"Yes, sir." Matt had met the barrister in his father's company a number of times over the years but had never gotten to know the man well.

Medgar Thaylor kept offices in Mayfair, one of London's more affluent areas. Simply walking into the Georgian manor house that had been converted into several offices was daunting. Even Paul had appeared to be somewhat impressed by the surroundings.

In his early seventies, with a leonine head of hair, side whiskers and mustache, the barrister had sharp gray eyes that looked as though they could stop a battleship under full sail. Though the private offices were big and spacious, even with shelves of books and expensive oxblood furniture, Thaylor made everything else look small in comparison. He was over six feet tall and thick-bodied.

"Regarding the matter of your father's business affairs, I'm afraid I can't offer much good news there." Thaylor opened the journal before him. "Before he—I should say, before you and your father—lost your mother, Lord Brockton was a good businessman. He took the money he inherited from your grandfather and did very well for himself. During the last seven years, though, your father's predilection took him away from his businesses. I fear that in addition to inattention, some of those businesses may now have corrupt managers." He paused and looked sympathetic. "While the cat is away, the mice will play, or so the story goes. Good men left your father's employ due to his inattentions, and they were not replaced by like-minded ones."

Matt nodded. "What do you think I should do?"

The barrister sighed. "In my opinion, you might be better served selling those businesses off before they're able to make a pauper of you. You could keep the family home and live quite comfortably for a long time on what you could make by conservatively investing the profits. That would be something."

"Perhaps," Paul said, speaking for the first time since introductions were made. "But that is not what Lord Brockton, Matt's father, intended. Nor is it what Lord Brockton now wishes to do."

Matt did not want to see everything his father had built vanish as a result of his enemies' machinations. The idea was intolerable. But he hadn't known—and still did not know—if that loss could be prevented.

"No," Thaylor agreed. He eyed Paul more deliberately, as if getting a better measure of him. "You are Lord Desmond's son."

"Yes," Paul agreed. "I am also an entrepreneur in my own right. More importantly in this moment, I am Matt's good friend."

"I see." Thaylor leaned back in his chair.

"While he lacks suitable training in these ventures," Paul continued, "Matt does not lack the capacity for learning how to handle them. I believe he can step into his own in these matters."

Thaylor waited.

"Lord Brockton has asked me to act on his behalf regarding the management of his holdings," Paul said.

"Do you trust this man with your financial well-being?" Thaylor asked, shifting his attention back to Matt.

"I trust Paul with my life," Matt replied without hesitation.

Thaylor leaned forward again and regarded Paul with his keen gray eyes. "What you're considering undertaking is no easy thing, Master Chadwick-Standish."

Paul gave the barrister a slight grin. "If it were, the task would be dull and uninteresting." He rolled his walking stick between his palms. "I choose to look upon this as an opportunity, not a hardship."

"And what do you get out of this?"

"What do you mean?" Paul asked, taken aback.

"In the matter of financial recompense."

"I don't expect to be paid for my involvement," Paul protested. "I am Matt's friend."

"As am I," Thaylor said. "Yet I get paid for my

services. As should you." The barrister flicked his keen glance at Matt. "And you should pay him. A percentage of profits will suit nicely, I should think."

Matt and Paul swapped looks.

"All right," Matt said.

"That sounds acceptable," Paul added, looking impressed, "and it provides me ample motive to take whatever steps I deem necessary to deal with those men who have seen fit to take advantage of the previous Lord Brockton."

"Fine. Then I'll have the papers drawn up and wish the both of you the best of luck." Thaylor made a notation in his personal journal.

"Mr. Thaylor," Matt said. "Did my father ever mention Lucius Creighdor?"

A wary look darkened the barrister's eyes. "Yes. On a number of occasions."

"In what regard?"

"There was bad blood between your father and Mr. Creighdor."

"Why?"

Thaylor leaned back in his chair, clearly not happy. "Your father was convinced that, in some fashion, Mr. Creighdor was involved in your mother's death."

Pain thudded into Matt's heart. "What do you think?"

"There was nothing to tie Mr. Creighdor to your mother's death, Lord Brockton. Owing to your father's position and the relationship he enjoyed with the Queen's court, Scotland Yard looked into the matter."

Matt tried to stop himself but failed. The words were out of his mouth almost at the instant he thought them. "The Scotland Yard investigators could have been bribed."

Sadness showed in Thaylor's eyes. "Your father, rest his soul, made that same accusation. It only earned him the ire of the very people he had gone to for help. This was not a conspiracy, Lord Brockton. God forgive me my bluntness, but it was the murder of one poor woman—may her soul be at rest—who was simply in the wrong place at the wrong time.

"And my father's death? Can you explain that away as diligently?"

"Your father was a most careful man when it came to munitions," Thaylor continued. "While he may have had weapons in that flat as the Scotland Yard inspectors maintain, I know that explosion was not of his causing."

"My father was murdered, Mr. Thaylor," Matt declared, "as surely as was my mother. I believe the same person killed both of them, but I have no proof. However, should I ever come into possession of proof, I may find that the authorities are reluctant to listen to me."

The gray eyes caught fire as they gleamed in the lamplight. "Then, should you find proof, I will help make people listen to you, Lord Brockton. As God is my witness, I shall do that very thing no matter who this man or these men shall be. For your father's memory, and for the courage I see in the young man standing before me."

"Thank you, Mr. Thaylor." Matt offered his hand and found it engulfed in the barrister's. He was surprised at the iron grip.

"But be careful," the barrister urged. "I would like to have a few years with you so that I might get to know you better."

Outside and once more on the street, Matt discovered that some of the fog and dreary weather that habitually plagued London in the fall had burned away. Weak sunlight cast pale shadows of the buildings on the cobblestones. Voices swelled to fill the streets and alleys, and small crowds paused before windows advertising the latest fashions in London and abroad.

The change in weather lifted Matt's spirits as he walked along with Paul at his side. But it took only a glimpse of the gargoyle grinning down from a nearby building to remind him that disaster still loomed.

"Well," Paul said brightly, "the discussion with your barrister went rather better than I expected. Especially when you decided to lay bare your soul."

"We're going to need allies, Paul. And

Medgar Thaylor is a powerful man in the right circles in London."

Paul sighed. "True. But you were taking a frightful chance telling him as much as you did."

"Not as big of a chance as we are taking merely walking the street."

Paul tapped his walking stick on the cobblestones. "Nonsense. This is London. The greatest city in the world. Not the countryside. People are safe to stroll the streets. Creighdor wouldn't dare send his lackeys after us here."

"My father dies in Lodon. And a gargoyle could fall from the rooftops on our heads and smash the life from us," Matt pointed out. "Who's to say that it wasn't an accident? Do you mark where gargoyles are and aren't? I certainly don't, though I will make an attempt to do so from now on."

Uncomfortably, Paul glanced up at the gargoyle grinning down from the building they passed. "It hasn't happened yet."

"That troubles me, though. I'd like to know why. It can't be merely because they think I have my father's diary, can it?"

"Well—and here I'm trying not to sound like some cheap braggart bending his elbow at a pub—I think part of your continued survival has to do with the fact that you've kept excellent company over the last two days."

Matt glanced at his friend.

"I'm referring to myself, of course." Paul smiled.

"Of course. Very wise of me, isn't it?"

Paul shrugged and adjusted his tie. "Killing the son of a somewhat public madman who has just committed suicide, at least in the eyes of the average citizen, might not draw too much attention. Other than a sympathetic cluck and a knowing elbow to the ribs of a mate. But killing the son of Lord Desmond? That would take some rather fancy footwork."

"Those men at the estate were willing to kill you."

Paul frowned. "That was there. Possibly they were thinking of blaming you."

Matt walked in silence for a time, then spoke quietly. "Creighdor killed my father. And he controls impossible creatures we don't yet understand. I find it hard to believe he is without resources."

"Then why let you live?"

"I don't know. That's part of what we have to find out, so we can use his motives to our advantage." Matt gazed around, wary and weary. "While we were at breakfast this morning, after the trip to the Fabulous Harn Museum, I formed a strategy."

"Yes?"

"We need to find out more about the ketch that brought the shipment in two nights ago. The one my father learned of from Mr. Peabody."

"*Saucy Lass*?"

"Yes. If she's not one of Creighdor's vessels,

we might get the cargo or one of the crew to talk about the cargo that night."

"I don't see that Creighdor would use a ship for anything important that wasn't his lock, stock, and barrel. I know that I wouldn't."

"But we haven't asked."

"True. And the possibility definitely bears looking into." Paul sighed. "First Gabriel and now you have seized upon something I should have thought of."

"You've had your head full of finding out about my father's business interests."

"Yes, well, in my opinion that is no excuse. Usually I am far more clever."

As Matt stepped off the curb to cross the next alley, six men in suits walked out of the alley. The men were big and blocky and didn't appear any too comfortable in the clothing that made them part of the Mayfair neighborhood. They blocked Paul and Matt's passage.

Matt came to a standstill but raised his clenched fists before him. Paul pulled at his arm, but Matt refused to run.

The man leading the group moved his long coat slightly, just enough to reveal the big, dark revolver he held in his hand. His gap-toothed smile split his moon-shaped face and made his curled mustache jiggle. No mirth lighted his pale blue eyes.

"Put down yer hands, boy," the man threatened as he patted his weapon. "Don't want passersby thinkin' yer bein' held up an' go runnin' for a copper. Otherwise I'd have to blow yer guts out an' leave ye here to die." He waggled the gun slightly. "Ye 'ave me word on that."

Chapter 10

Matt froze, calculating his chances at avoiding a bullet before he could reach the confusion of the street.

"Ye'd be too slow, laddie," the mustached man promised, still smiling. He shifted the concealed pistol slightly, enough to draw Matt's attention. "I been at this 'ere business a long time, an' I'll never be taken by some wet-behind-the-ears greenie."

Before Matt could move, one of the other men seized Paul and yanked him back into the alley's shadows. If anyone out on the street saw the action, no one did anything.

This is Mayfair, Matt thought desperately as fear flooded his mind and tried to drown his reason. *This kind of thing doesn't go on here. Not in broad daylight.*

But it was today.

"So what do ye say, laddie?" the man asked

with good-natured ease. "Come along into the alley there fer a set-to? Or mayhap ye want to try yer luck at runnin'?" The grin grew wider. "Ye won't get far. I promise ye that. A bullet 'tween yer shoulder blades'll do fer ye. An' yer friend there?" He nodded at Paul. "Why, we'll slit his gullet an' leave 'im to die there in that alley. An' if ye was lucky enough to get away, which ye won't be, ye can tell 'is mum 'ow 'e died like a stuck pig on account of ye."

All right, Matt thought, *maybe we'll have to consider how hard Creighdor is willing to try to take me alive.*

"Did Creighdor send you?" Matt's heart thumped like a blacksmith's hammer. Reluctantly, he lowered his fists.

"Now see there? Ye're already goin' at this game wrong. It's me what's gonna be askin' the questions an' tellin' ye 'ow things is gonna be. Ye're just gonna do as ye're told." The man jerked his chin toward the alley but his eyes never left Matt's. "Get on with yerself. I 'asn't got all bloody day to be about this 'ere."

Paul stood within the alley, pressed up tight against the wall behind him. The man who had manhandled him leaned on him with one big hand placed squarely in the middle of his chest. Paul stared at Matt anxiously.

"All right," Matt said.

"Good. There's a bright lad. Now drop them 'ands."

Matt stepped into the alley. He halted only when the big man seized his shoulder and brought him to a stop.

Out on the street carriages and coaches rumbled by. Even a few pedestrians passed, giving the group of men a curious look, then hurrying on.

"Now then," the big man said as he stepped in front of Matt just out of arm's reach, "let's talk."

"Did Creighdor send you?" Matt demanded.

The big man backhanded Matt before he saw it coming. Pain exploded inside Matt's head from the initial blow, then again from the stone wall his head bounced off of. His knees went weak and he thought for a moment he was going to fall.

"I ain't got me much patience," the man warned, "so ye'll want to go easy on tryin' it."

Matt steadied himself and wiped a hand across his bloody mouth. He studied the man, memorizing everything he could about him.

"If I see you again," Matt promised in a low, cold voice, "I'll know you. And I'll kill you."

The man chuckled, and the two other men joined in.

"Well now," he said, "I feel all properly threatened, I do. Quiverin' in me boots an' faint of 'eart, I am."

Matt felt the heat of his anger and helplessness color his face. "Just so you're warned."

The man's face hardened into a sneer. "Ye got somethin' my employer wants," he said. "I aims to get it for 'im."

"What do you want?"

The man shook his head. "Don't play with me, lad. Ye'll regret it."

"I'm not playing. I don't know what you want. I don't even know who you're working for."

The big man grimaced and labored for a long moment over a decision. "I was told to fetch a book. The man tellin' me, 'e said you'd know what book."

"I don't know what you're talking about. What man?"

The man's blow nearly knocked Matt senseless. His head slammed against the wall and he dropped to one knee.

"Ye're trying me patience, boy. That ain't a smart thing to do. I've precious little on a good day, an' this ain't a good day."

Matt forced himself to stand. He spat blood on his attacker's suit jacket. Just as the man was about to hit him again, a hansom cab turned from the street and entered the alley.

The men looked uneasy.

Hope flooded Matt's brain; he thought some Good Samaritan had seen what was going on and was prepared to help.

The man flattened Matt against the wall with a forearm. "There ain't nothin' there for ye, boy."

The cab came to a stop. The driver was a mousy man of indeterminate years. He climbed down and opened the cab's door.

A slim well-built man in his mid-twenties stepped from the cab. He made a show of pulling on kidskin gloves. His suit was dark and tailored.

"Lord Brockton," the man said in a cultured voice that held a trace of an accent.

Staring at him, Matt felt certain he knew the other's identity. The voice sounded a lot like one he'd heard the night he and his father had confronted *Saucy Lass*.

"I am Lucius Creighdor," the man announced. His words held menace. His hair was long, held back in a jeweled queue, and loose bangs hung down into his dark eyes. His face was thin and sallow. His thin mustache bled down into a manicured goatee. His teeth showed white and clean and sharp.

"You killed my father," Matt growled hoarsely.

"Yes."

The chilling bluntness of the answer momentarily paralyzed Matt. He hadn't anticipated the callous response. He lunged from the wall but the big man held him back.

"Murderer!" Matt yelled.

The man hit him in the stomach, knocking the wind out of him.

Creighdor put a cautionary finger to his thin, cruel lips in a theatrical gesture. "Shhhh! If you draw attention to this little tête-à-tête, rest assured I'll not hesitate to have your friend's life snuffed as quickly and thoughtlessly as a candle flame."

Paul's captor put a broad-bladed knife to his throat.

Creighdor smiled, but the effort was without mirth. "Your choice, young Lord Brockton. I'll not suffer another generation of trouble from your family. Choose well."

Matt swallowed hard and tasted blood. "What do you want?"

"Your father's book."

"He had a lot of books."

"Don't be churlish. Neither of us have the time for that. And your friend has even less time."

"The book he had written about you."

"Yes."

"It burned. In the fire."

Creighdor nodded. "That copy, most certainly. I want the other copy. Or copies. I want to know what your father knew. Your father was a smart man. A cunning man. Unfortunately, he was a brave man. That, in the end, was what got him killed."

Matt debated, not knowing what to say. A line of blood ran down Paul's neck from where the knife blade had broken his flesh.

"Come, come," Creighdor urged. "I know he told you where it was that night. He must have."

You killed him too quickly, Matt thought, but he said nothing.

"Macleod," Creighdor said to the biggest man in the alley, "blind the other one."

"Yes, Mr. Creighdor."

A wave of sickness pulsed through Matt. He couldn't bear to watch Paul be hurt in such a manner. However, if he admitted he didn't know if the second book even existed, Matt felt certain both their lives would be forfeit. He had no choice; he knew he had to act.

The man guarding Matt turned to Macleod, evidently wanting to watch Paul's maiming.

Knowing the pistol was the most dangerous component in the confrontation, Matt grabbed the weapon and the man's coat all at the same time. He slipped his finger inside the trigger guard, pushed the barrel into the face of the man holding Paul, and squeezed the trigger. The bullet struck the man in the head. Dead already or dying, the man released Paul and dropped to the ground before the rolling echo of the shot passed from the alley.

Abandoning all civilized pretext at fighting, Matt smashed his forehead against his own captor's face hard enough to partially stun himself with the impact. The man's nose broke and gushed blood. Before his opponent could recover, Matt kicked him in the groin as hard as he could. As the man sank to the alley floor, Matt curled his fingers into a fist and drove it into

Macleod's face, putting all of his shoulder behind the punch and twisting his hip to get as much power into the blow as he could.

Momentarily dazed, Macleod dropped to his knees and sprawled forward. A pistol fell to the cobblestones beneath him. Unable to reach the weapon without stepping into his opponent's grasp, Matt kicked the pistol and sent it skidding out toward the street. The weapon hung for just a moment on a sewer grate at one side of the alley, then toppled over and fell through.

The fourth man drew a long knife from his hip and started for Matt. Paul lifted his walking stick and whacked the man in the throat. Temporarily choked by the unexpected blow, the man staggered away.

Creighdor's driver also had a knife. Paul twisted his walking stick and bared the sword blade hidden inside. He slashed at the man, catching the knife and cutting the man's jacket and shirtfront. The man stepped back, forced into motion by the sword point suddenly hovering in his face.

Matt turned toward Creighdor.

Creighdor grinned. "Another time, young Lord Brockton. This is much too public a place for this level of exposure. I'll settle with you at a later date." He raised his voice. "Mr. Macleod, do carry on as we agreed."

Matt surged forward, but Creighdor moved

with almost impossible quickness and kicked him in the face. He staggered back.

Creighdor vaulted into the cab's seat, gathered the reins, and urged the horse into a gallop. The animal's hooves rang against the cobblestones.

Refusing to give up, Matt reached for the cab as it passed. The smooth finish of the side sped under his fingertips. Then it was gone.

"Matt," Paul called.

Around them, Macleod and his cronies gathered. Macleod searched for another pistol, cursing Matt vigorously.

The cab driver stood in front of Paul with his knife in his fist.

"Run," Paul suggested. He stood in an *en garde* position, his left arm tucked behind him and every movement of his body following his right arm and right toe. It was immediately apparent that he could easily run the man through where he stood.

The man retreated, but only as far as the alley mouth. Six other men joined him there. They bared knives and pistols. Evidently the first group had brought friends.

"Alive," Macleod cried as he pushed against the alley wall and forced himself to his feet. "'E's not supposed to be killed. Ye can kill 'is bloody friend all ye want."

Matt joined Paul. Together they faced the crowd and slowly backed away.

"They're willing to kill me," Paul said, "so I get to cast the deciding vote on whether we stay to fight or to run."

"All right." Matt's hand and head throbbed painfully. Creighdor had already disappeared out into the street.

"We run," Paul said. "Now." He turned and fled.

Matt stayed on his friend's heels as they ran toward the other end of the alley.

The men gave chase. If the pursuit had taken place in the East End, a howling mob wouldn't have drawn much attention. The people who lived in the East End accepted trouble and hardship as familiar neighbors.

But this was Mayfair. A man in Mayfair might have an altercation with a business associate or a holdup man, but this many people involved in violence would draw attention and some kind of intervention from the authorities.

At the other end of the alley, Matt turned right, running into the oncoming traffic. He lost his footing for a moment and ended up in front of a carriage. He put his hands out, caught hold of the horse's harness and barely managed to pull himself out from under the iron-shod hooves in the nick of time. His face pressed against the damp hide of the horse's neck and the musk of the animal clung to him as he hurled himself away.

The carriage jerked to a halt as the frightened

horse reared. The driver cursed after Matt, then fell silent as the men pursuing Paul and Matt rounded the corner of the alley, exploding into view.

Matt stayed to the middle of the street, keeping the line of carriages and cabs between himself and the group of men pounding down the sidewalk after Paul.

Paul ran quickly and carried the walking stick case in one hand and the naked sword in the other. He was fleet of foot and was gradually outdistancing most of the men in the pack. But two were seriously closing the gap and would overtake him before the end of the block.

Desperate, Matt charged back into the path of the next carriage, a large brougham built to hold up to six passengers which wouldn't easily be stopped. The horses wore blinders, allowing them to see only what was immediately in front of them. Matt counted on that restricted vision for his hasty plan.

In front of the horses, almost close enough to touch them, Matt threw his arms wide and shouted, looking as big and as threatening as he could.

Startled, the team of horses shied and tried to fight clear of him, dodging to their left and into the path of the group charging on Paul's heels. Seeing the new group of people, the horses attempted to stop again, but with the weight of the heavy brougham pushing them forward, couldn't.

The lead horse smashed into the lead runner and knocked him back. Two other men smacked into the confused tangle of animals, carriage, and men. But the others quickly rounded the mess and continued on their way.

Matt ran through the street, watching as other carriage drivers halted their animals or pulled to the side before he reached them. There was no sign of Creighdor.

"Matt," Paul yelled as he caught up to a hansom cab whose driver had stopped to wonder at all the confusion.

Driving his feet against the cobblestones, Matt caught up to Paul and the cab.

Paul brandished money like a weapon at the driver. "Get us out of here. Now."

"All right, guv'nor," the hack driver agreed, snatching the money from Paul's hand.

Matt and Paul were inside the cab and rolling along the street well before their attackers gathered themselves and regrouped. With all the attention they were getting from the passersby and the street traffic, the men chose to retreat into the alleys.

"That was too close," Paul commented.

Matt nodded. "This can mean only one thing."

"What?"

"We must be getting close to something. Creighdor is getting nervous. Otherwise he would never have confronted us today." Matt paused. "I want to go after Creighdor."

"Going after Creighdor is impossible. Even if we were able to find him, what would you do?"

"I'd kill him."

"You'd never get close to him."

Matt wanted to yell and break something. Anything.

"More than that," Paul added soberly, "you don't know if killing Creighdor will stop everything your father feared would happen to England."

Matt made himself breathe out. "I know."

"We've surprised him," Paul said. "Take solace in that. We have struck a blow. And we've brought him out of wherever he's been hiding. We'll bring him out again."

"Creighdor is afraid of whatever is in my father's book."

"I believe so as well."

"We need to find that book."

"We will."

"I just wish I knew it existed."

"Creighdor feels that it must. So do Gabriel and I. We aren't wrong."

Matt thought for a moment, regaining his breath. "I think it's time to find the ship's captain. The one who was the master of *Saucy Lass*. Whether we find out anything or not, Creighdor is going to know we're on his trail."

"That could be dangerous."

Matt looked at his friend. "It's already dangerous, Paul. I think it's time we became dangerous ourselves."

Baynard Stebbins, ship's captain and once commander of *Saucy Lass*, proved relatively easy to find. Paul's contacts within the shipping business came in handily for their search.

Within three hours, the two friends discovered that Stebbins had been summarily discharged from his duties aboard *Saucy Lass* the previous morning. Paul's contacts indicated only that Lucius Creighdor had grown unhappy with the man and had chosen to release him. The two left word of their whereabouts with one of the urchins Gabriel had left to ferry messages.

Twenty minutes and a swift cab ride later, Matt and Paul found Stebbins at the Compass Rose, a small pub in Southwark on the south side of the Thames River. Southwark was a blight on London, an area filled with warehouses and slums, where poor people lived hard lives brimming with unrelenting heartache and merciless circumstances.

Dressed in their fine clothes and arriving by hired cab, Matt and Paul stood out in the neighborhood at once.

The Compass Rose was redolent of cheap pipe tobacco and cheaper rum and ale. Years of smoke, spills, and hard use stained the dark walls and scarred the floor. Heavy drapes covered the windows and blocked out the sunlight, while lanterns created dim pools of light at a few tables.

Paul stepped to the bar, where a man stood wiping glasses with a towel. "Pardon me. I'm looking for Captain Stebbins. Captain Baynard Stebbins."

"Are you debt collectors then?" the man asked, taking in their suits.

Though their clothes were slightly dirty and torn from the fight with Creighdor's men, Matt was grimly aware both of them were still far overdressed for the pub.

The barman continued talking in a threatening voice without giving Paul or Matt a chance to answer. "This 'ere's me pub, an' no place of yours if that's what you're about. I'll not 'ave no workin' man what's down on 'is luck troubled by the likes of you whilst 'e's tryin' for a moment's peace."

"We're not debt collectors," Paul said. "We've come here to interview Captain Stebbins for a job."

The pub owner looked at their suits again. Then he raised his voice. "Anyone in 'ere name o' Stebbins what wants to talk with these two 'ere? Says they come 'ere lookin' to give out a job."

Matt looked around the room. For a moment the silence held, and he was afraid they'd come at a time when Stebbins wasn't there.

A man in his thirties turned up the lantern on his table so the light grew brighter. "I'm Stebbins."

Paul thanked the pub owner and left coins on the scarred countertop.

Matt's heart sped up as they made their way to the table. "You're Captain Baynard Stebbins?"

The man was small and compact. His side-whiskers were neatly trimmed, dark red like his combed hair. His face was pinched and drawn, weathered by the wind and the sun and harsh circumstances that had left two old scars half hidden by the seams in his leathery cheek. He was fresh shaven despite the fact that he'd lost his ship and had obviously settled into the Compass Rose to drink his cares and the night away.

"Aye." Stebbins gestured to the chairs on the other side of the table. "If'n we're gonna talk business, 'ave a sit. Gonna get uncomfortable for all of us with ye two a-standin' there an' me a-lookin' up at ye the whole time." He paused. "Unless ye only 'ave a short stay."

"Thank you." Matt pulled out one of the chairs and prepared to sit.

"You'll excuse my forwardness," Paul said, "but could we see some proof you actually are Captain Baynard Stebbins?"

The man grinned a little and reached inside his shirt. "I likes a man what's careful. What's yer name?"

"Paul Chadwick-Standish."

Matt watched the captain's face for any sign that he recognized Paul's name. There was none, but a ship's captain was trained to show little or no emotion during the worst circumstances.

Stebbins pulled out his seaman's papers. "I 'ave me papers right 'ere. I'll be a-wanting to see some identification from ye." He spread the papers on the tabletop.

Paul quickly brought out his own papers and showed them.

"An who might yer frien' be?" Stebbins asked, looking at Matt.

As he sat in the chair, Matt wondered if the captain might remember him from the incident two nights ago. The night had been dark and foggy, but that didn't mean he hadn't been seen.

"For the moment, my friend remains nameless." Paul sat beside Matt.

Stebbins growled a curse but looked over Paul's papers. "I don't like doin' business with them what I don't know."

Paul took an envelope from inside his jacket and placed it in the center of the table. The paper envelope looked white and new against the stained tabletop.

"Inside that envelope is twenty quid," Paul said.

Eyeing the envelope suspiciously, Stebbins asked, "Fer what?"

"For simply taking the time to listen to our proposition." Paul tapped his walking stick against the floor.

Stebbins took the envelope, glanced inside it,

and shoved it inside his jacket along with his papers. "Aye. Ye've got me attention. But I ain't gonna listen to ye jabber all night. Get on with it."

"That's fine, Captain Stebbins," Paul said. "My friend and I are prepared to offer you a ship."

"I'm a man a-lookin' fer a ship." Stebbins gave a brief nod. "I reckon ye 'eard what happened, otherwise ye wouldn't be 'ere now." He tapped the envelope inside his jacket. "But ye don't pay a man twenty quid to offer 'im a job. Leastways, I never before 'ad somethin' offered to me in such a fashion."

"There's a first time for everything." Paul grinned, but there was little humor in the effort. "But you're right. My friend and I do want more than just to hire a ship's captain."

Stebbins sipped rum from his glass. "I'm still listenin'."

Matt felt ashamed when he saw the hunger in the man's eyes. Stebbins was a ship's captain without a ship. Matt knew from his experience with the captains his father employed that there was no worse fate outside of death for a confirmed sailing man. The offer of a ship's captaincy was legitimate. Even with his father's failing resources, Matt could make that happen, and would.

"I want to know about the cargo *Saucy Lass* brought into London two nights ago."

Stebbins shrugged. "Not much to tell. Ye can

'ave yourself a look at the records in the Customs 'ouse if'n ye want."

Matt could no longer sit idly by. He desperately wanted to question Stebbins about Creighdor and his father's death. It was possible Stebbins knew about Lord Brockton's murder because it happened so quickly after the confrontation on the docks.

"We're not talking about the cargo declared on the manifests in the Customs House," Matt said. "We want to know about the undeclared cargo you carried aboard that ship."

Stebbins leaned back in his chair and crossed his arms over his chest. "I don't see that that's any business of yers."

"I'm making it my business." Matt stared into the man's eyes.

"My friend is the one with the ship," Paul said. "He can make you captain, or we can walk away from this table. You pick."

"This could be a trick," Stebbins said. "Ye could be testin' me loyalty."

"It's no trick," Matt said. "I want to confirm what you already know. That's the price for a captaincy today." He didn't actually know whose body was inside the box Scanlon had picked up, but he did know it was a body. Every bit of information he could assemble against Creighdor counted.

Paul reached into his other jacket pocket and took out another sheaf of papers. He opened them so Stebbins could see them. "Have a look at this."

Stebbins peered at the papers. "This 'ere's a contract."

"That's right," Paul said. "And it guarantees you a year's salary once you're signed on as ship's captain. This contract is legal and binding. Just awaiting your signature. To show you that my friend is serious in his offer."

"Yer friend still don't 'ave a name," Stebbins observed.

"I undersigned that agreement," Paul said. "That makes me just as responsible as he is. You'll get your ship, Captain Stebbins. *If* we get the answers we want."

Matt forced himself to sit silently as his friend hammered out the details of the offer to Stebbins. He was amazed at how good a negotiator Paul was. Evidently he had learned a lot through his investments and time spent doing business.

In the past, Matt had always considered those subjects boring. Money hadn't meant anything to him. Now he recognized that capital wealth was another weapon in his arsenal against Lucius Creighdor.

Stebbins rubbed his jaw and thought for a moment. "I want ye to know that Lucius Creighdor did me fer a bad turn. I don't want ye thinkin' I turn quick against people. But Creighdor's got this 'ere comin'. I didn't do nothin' that warranted 'im takin' *Saucy Lass* from me.

That cargo ye're talkin' about?" He shook his head. "Creighdor thought I told people about it. But I didn't. I don't know 'ow come that madman to show up at the docks that night, but I do know it weren't my fault. Creighdor chose not to see it that way."

"The cargo," Paul pressed.

Stebbins took another sip of his drink and said in a low voice, "'Twas a body."

"Whose body?" Paul asked.

"Don't rightly know. Didn't ask. Wasn't told. Aboard *Saucy Lass*, I was paid for not knowin' things sometimes." Stebbins looked defensive. "Not knowin' sometimes pays more'n knowin'. Ever' ship's captain works that way. Either for 'imself an' his mates, or for 'is employers. That's just 'ow business gets done."

"Where did you ship the body from?"

"Egypt. That's where we picked it up. Creighdor had it there waitin' on us. We just smuggled it in with the rest of the cargo." Stebbins shook his head. "I didn't like 'avin' the bloody thing aboard. Neither did the crew."

"The body was in Egypt?" Paul asked.

"Aye. An' a frightful thing gettin' it was too. For all we knowed, them what got the thing brought a curse from the tomb. 'Eard about how them curses 'as killed lots of folks. An' there were some in the crew that kept waitin' fer that body to come back to life an' kill us all durin' the whole voyage."

"A curse?" Paul asked.

Understanding, Matt said, "Captain Stebbins is saying they brought back a mummy."

"A mummy?" Paul looked even more perplexed.

Stebbins smiled. "That's right. That's what we brung back. One of them bandage-wrapped corpses in one of them stone boxes. That's what Creighdor 'ad us fetch in such an 'urry."

Chapter 11

Why would Creighdor want two mummies?" Paul asked. "For that matter, why would he want one? From everything I've discovered about him, he's not a man with frivolous interests. There's no profit in owning a mummy. And if he wanted two, why wouldn't he buy a second from whoever sold him the one in Egypt instead of trying to buy the one at the Fabulous Harn Museum?"

Matt stepped out into the street in front of the Compass Rose and flagged down a hansom cab creaking and clattering by on the cobblestones. It was late afternoon and they'd left Stebbins inside the pub still drinking but with a freshly inked contract in his pocket. The man would have a ship by the end of the month.

"Because something makes that mummy special," Matt said.

"What?" Paul sounded exasperated.

"I don't know." Matt reached for the cab's door. Before he touched the handle, though, the door opened. Looking up, he spotted Gabriel seated in a corner of the cab.

"'Ello, 'ello," Gabriel greeted with a broad smile, leaning forward and resting his elbows on his knees. He gestured to the opposite seat with his hand. "Step right in, me fine young gentlemen."

Paul peered into the cab's interior. "What are you doing here?"

"I got your message sayin' you was off for these parts." Gabriel nodded toward the rear of the cab where the driver was. "So I asked Meacham there to stay in the neighborhood. In case you needed a quick getaway or I needed to know if you'd run afoul of trouble."

"That explains Meacham's presence," Paul declared. "What brings you here?"

"'Ad a bit of luck, I did," Gabriel declared happily. "Or, p'rhaps I should say, *we've* 'ad a bit of luck. Course, one man calls it luck while another man knows I been workin' to make this happen, so maybe 'tweren't luck at all."

Matt clambered into the cab and sat on the bench opposite Gabriel. Paul crowded in beside him.

"What luck?" Matt asked.

"I found our mysterious 'indu lad, I did. Pays to be diligent an' ever resourceful, no mistakin' that. An' me an' mine are good at what we does."

He theatrically polished his nails on his jacket. "The lad did not immediately return to 'is 'ome. 'E ran errands around the city after lookin' over the museum an' us this mornin', an' 'e kept a weather eye peeled for someone 'e knew shouldn't be around while 'e did hit. 'E's a cagey one, that one is. Whatever 'e's up to, 'e's lookin' out for 'isself just fine. Course, 'e was no match for the likes of me an' me lads."

"What did you find out about him?"

"'Is name. Where 'e lives. Family name's Chaudhary."

"He didn't see you, did he?"

Gabriel frowned. "Not on your life, guv'nor."

Paul tapped his walking stick. "It might well be our lives, you know."

"An' mine," Gabriel countered. He leaned back in the seat. "We're all safe as we can be. As safe as we were this mornin', leastways."

"Where's Donovan?" Matt asked.

"Up makin' 'is rounds, 'e is. 'E's steppin' lively, 'e is."

"Has he been to the museum today?"

Gabriel shook his head. "Not once. Which is odd after all them times yestiddy. But I suppose there's a reason. We'll sniff it out soon enough."

"But you have someone following him?" Paul asked.

"Of course." Gabriel knuckled his eyes.

For the first time Matt saw how tired his friend was. With everything that was going on,

Gabriel couldn't have slept at all. "You should get some rest."

Gabriel cocked his head and grinned. "I will, Matt. I will. After we can put this matter in a safe place for a bit. There's too much we still don't know, an' you're in some fine pickle, I promise you. I 'eard Creighdor 'as a pack of wolves out lookin' for the two of you."

"They already found us," Paul said.

Gabriel raised an eyebrow. "I didn't 'ear about that."

"We got away," Paul said. "That's why we're still here."

"Evidently Creighdor is feelin' some anxiousness. I've put me nose to the ground, I 'ave, an' I learned that 'ere lately 'e's been buyin' up gamblin' notes from bookmakers. Only the notes of them what's in the House of Lords. An' their sons, of course."

Matt considered that but couldn't make sense of it. "Why would Creighdor do that?"

"For blackmail purposes," Paul answered immediately. "There can be no other reason. From what I've seen of Creighdor's profits, he doesn't need to buy into hard-luck gamblers even for shillings on the pound."

Gabriel touched his nose and smiled. "Mayhap I should give some thought to bein' an investor." He leaned back and knocked on the coach roof, raising his voice to address the driver. "Let's go, Meacham, before somebody thinks we're just sittin' 'ere waitin' for these two fine young gentlemen to get robbed."

"Where are we going?" Paul asked.

"I thought I'd take you by the Chaudhary place," Gabriel said. "You can give it the eyeball an' decide what you want to do after that."

"Do you think that's wise?" Paul asked.

Gabriel peered out the cab's window and smiled. "A lot wiser than the two of you comin' 'ere dressed as you are."

Thankfully, Histories and Antiquities was located in between Threadneedle Street and Cornhill Street near Bishopsgate. The little two-story shop was squeezed between a barrister's offices and a pub, just east of the imposing and somewhat threatening Bank of England. The area maintained sizeable markets, and several people traded and bought there every morning. At this time of afternoon, nearer to evening, all of the markets had closed, but most of the shops remained open.

Matt paid the cab driver, and they all stepped out in front of a hat shop across the street from the antiquities establishment that Gabriel said the young man had stepped into. Paul busied himself perusing the hat shop's wares with a practiced eye.

"It's an 'indu family what owns the place," Gabriel said softly. "The father's name is Narada Chaudhary. The son's name, the bloke what was watchin' us this mornin', is Jaijo. 'E's a right enough one. Never no trouble that I 'eard of. There's a mum, another son, an' three daughters. Jaijo is the oldest of 'em. They come from India sixteen years ago an' opened this shop six years ago. Before he got into the antiquities business, Narada Chaudhary was an entertainer at a circus an' a consultant for some of the museums an' antiquities shops 'ere in London. 'E was an antiquities man back 'ome. Did authentications, auctions, an' the like."

"An entertainer and a consultant?" Paul asked.

"Narada Chaudhary was a fakir. One of them blokes what can walk through fire, lay on a bed of nails, an' make a rope rise out of a wicker basket just by playin' a flute. But 'e got shut of that line of work soon as 'e could an' opened 'is own shop."

"What about criminal connections?" Matt asked.

Gabriel shook his head. "Near as I can find out—an' mind you, I ain't finished me lookin' yet—Chaudhary's business an' his ways of conductin' it are all clean as a whistle, they is. Seems a right 'onorable bloke."

"Honorable people don't spy on other people," Paul said.

"Oh?" Gabriel lifted his eyebrows. "I guess prolly 'onorable gents just 'ires other people to do hit for 'em, doesn't they?"

Paul shot Gabriel a disdainful look. "Honorable people hire experts to spy on people who have tried to harm them."

"Does Chaudhary have any mummies for sale?" Matt interrupted. "Perhaps their interest is not in us so much as our dealings at the Harn Museum."

"Don't know. 'Aven't put foot inside the shop meself."

"Then perhaps we should take a look." Matt walked across the street. Anger and excitement flared within him. There had to be a reason why Jaijo Chaudhary was watching their activities at the Fabulous Harn Museum. Maybe knowing Jaijo Chaudhary's reason would be enough to reveal what Creighdor and Donovan's interest in the mummy was. And maybe that would reveal what Roger Hunter's interest had been. Too many things were centering on the mummy for it not to have considerable import.

A handsome window, made up of many panes with the name of the shop hand-lettered across them, presented a view of beautiful vases, goblets, and statuary. All of them looked like modest pieces, and since they were not under heavy security, Matt felt certain the Chaudharys sold primarily curio pieces and tourist knick-knacks. They were mostly pieces of history for an armchair historian or enthusiast, nothing a thief could quickly turn into a profit.

The second story was obviously a home for

the Chaudhary family. Two little girls with bored eyes peered out one window at the street. Heavy drapes framed their faces. A woman's voice called out in a foreign language and the girls withdrew into the room.

Matt stepped onto the walk and went through the door, setting off a tiny brass bell that hung above to announce visitors. The sound was almost enough to make Matt jump out of his skin.

Inside, the shop was efficiently laid out. Short shelves filled the center space. Pieces crowded the open space. Taller shelves lined the walls, offering statuary, vases, books, maps, and handmade jewelry.

To the left stood the main counter, which was crowded with glass jars holding pipe tobacco and brightly colored hard candy. A man in his early fifties stood behind the counter.

The man stood five and a half feet tall. His face was too broad for his narrow build. Swarthy skin contrasted with his graying hair and beard. Round-lensed glasses rode low on his nose. He wore a black tie, white shirt with sleeve garters, and black pants.

"Good afternoon, young sirs," the man greeted in a deep, soft voice. He smiled hopefully. "Might I help you look for your heart's desire?" He spread his hands to include the room. "As you can see, I have many things."

"You're Narada Chaudhary?" Matt asked,

stepping up to the counter. He was taller and heavier than the shopkeeper.

"I am he." The shopkeeper didn't look flustered, but he didn't act overly curious either. He didn't demand to know how Matt knew him.

He also hasn't asked who I am, Matt realized.

"Were you looking for anything in particular, sahib?" Narada asked.

"I want to know about the mummy at the Fabulous Harn Museum," Matt said, working off his hunch.

After a flicker of hesitation, a brief pause that wouldn't have been noticeable under normal circumstances, Narada said, "That is not my property, sir. You would be better served asking the owners of the museum."

"I think you know more about the mummy than they do." Matt put an accusatory edge in his voice. "You may even know as much as a police inspector named George Donovan and a man named Lucius Creighdor."

Narada blinked at him for a moment. "How would I know these things?"

"Your son Jaijo was there this morning. He was watching us. Unless he's doing this on his own and you knew nothing about it. Maybe he's the expert on that particular mummy. In that case, I'll want to talk to him." Matt stared at the man.

Narada hesitated. He removed his glasses and cleaned the lenses with a soft cloth from his pocket. He put them back on and looked at Matt. "I had been wondering after this morning if you would come here, Lord Brockton. Jaijo said he was certain you saw him, but he didn't know you would be able to track him back here."

Gabriel immediately stepped back. The way he shifted his hand to his coat pocket told Matt that the young thief hadn't come unarmed. Gabriel kept his eyes moving as if expecting a trap.

"You know me?" Matt asked. He immediately worried he'd stepped into a trap and led his friends into it as well. The close call this morning had brought him the cold realization that he couldn't protect the people he was asking to risk their lives.

The man nodded. "I saw you with your father a few times."

Seeing that Narada wasn't reaching for a weapon, Matt relaxed a little. "When?"

"We were at public functions at the same time. Nothing important. We weren't introduced and I'm quite sure you paid no attention to me."

"How did you know my father?"

"We were friends. I like to think we were good friends, though not close friends."

"I know my father's friends," Matt challenged. But he knew in his heart that this was no longer true. He and his father had lived very separate lives over the past few years.

Narada shook his head. "Not all of your

father's friends, Lord Brockton. You don't know me. There are others."

The statement spun through Matt's head and sent out tendrils of fear. "What others?"

"Men your father shared interests with."

"What interests did my father share with you?"

Narada waved a hand at the shop. "What you see before you. History. Antiquities."

"My father was never a collector of other people's histories," Matt stated. "The things we had in our house he retrieved himself from the places he'd been. All of them have specific stories behind them. My father's stories." And that was true, though Matt did not know the stories behind all the pieces.

"I know."

"Then why did he talk to you?"

"On a consultation basis."

"What did he consult you about?"

Narada hesitated.

"Did one of those consultations concern the mummy at the Fabulous Harn Museum?"

"Yes. Your father did talk to me regarding that mummy."

"What did he want to know?"

"The mummy's history. Where it came from. How it came to be made. Who it was when the man lived."

Matt tried to take in everything he was being told, but it was too confusing. "My father was never interested in Egyptology."

"Not Egyptology," Narada agreed. "But he was interested in that mummy." He paused. "You know that fact is true, Lord Brockton, or you would not be here in my shop now."

Movement caught Matt's peripheral vision and pulled his attention to the right.

Wary and nervous, Jaijo Chaudhary stepped into the room. He carried a curved military sword. Perhaps he was only preparing the weapon for display, but Matt didn't think so. The young man held the sword with too much determination.

"Father," Jaijo said, never taking his eyes from Matt.

Narada gestured impatiently to his son. "Put that away. Everything is all right."

"Everything is *not* all right," Jaijo said, gazing at Matt, Paul, and Gabriel. "They should not be here. Their presence here is dangerous to us."

"Their presence here is dangerous to them as well as us." Chaudhary walked over to his son and gently took the sword away. "Lord Brockton was asking after his father's interest in the mummy."

Jaijo fixed Matt with his gaze. "What you know can get you killed."

"What I don't know," Matt countered, "has nearly gotten me killed three times. Twice, my friends' lives were at stake as well. I believe knowing more about what is going on is only going to improve my chances for survival."

"You don't know who you are facing," Jaijo said impatiently.

"I know who I'm facing. Lucius Creighdor and Josiah Scanlon." Matt held his gaze steady. "The men who murdered my mother and my father. If there are others, I will find them." He paused and hardened his voice. "If you are part of his organization, or in any way responsible for the deaths of my parents, I will bring you down as well."

"How dare you!" Jaijo started forward.

Narada placed a restraining hand against his son's chest. "No." He looked at his son. He spoke again, more quietly. "No. I will handle this."

Jaijo spoke in his native tongue, obviously very upset.

"In English," Narada admonished. "I will have them hear everything we say."

"He doesn't even know what he is talking about."

"Then we will help him understand." Narada glanced at Matt. "There may be things he can tell us that will help us in our own endeavors."

"We cannot trust them," Jaijo protested.

"We have no choice. Just as he had no choice in coming here."

"We could send them away."

"Jaijo, Lord Brockton was killed. Things are worse than I believed. We—your mother, your brother, and your sisters—are in much more danger than I realized."

"Lord Brockton killed himself," Jaijo said desperately. "That is what is in the newspapers."

"He was murdered," Matt said, though he felt certain the young man struggled only to convince himself how Roger Hunter had met his untimely fate.

Jaijo wheeled on Matt. "How can you say this?"

"Because," Matt said, "I was there when he was murdered. I saw it. My father did not take his own life through purpose or mishap. He was killed in front of me."

Silence filled the small shop for a moment. Then Narada left his son and walked to the front of the store. He locked the door, put up a closed sign, and pulled the shades down.

"Come," Narada said, gesturing to the back of the shop. "There is a workroom in the back. We can talk there."

Matt followed, knowing that Jaijo still did not trust him. But that was fine. He didn't trust the father and son either.

Chapter 12

"How much do you know?" Narada asked. He busied himself with pouring tea.

The workroom was small and compact. Shelves lined the walls, filled with items that obviously needed care and cleaning before they could be placed on the display stands in the outer shop. A rectangular table, partially covered by projects in different stages of cleaning and recovery, occupied the center of the room. Benches stood on either side of it, with a chair at either end.

"About what?" Matt asked.

Narada waved them to seats.

Matt took the seat at the other end of the table. Paul sat to his immediate right, and Gabriel declined a seat. The young thief stood near the door with his hands crossed over his chest. His right hand was tucked almost casually inside his jacket; Matt believed Gabriel gripped whatever weapon he'd brought to the meeting.

"About Creighdor and Scanlon." Narada returned to the table with the tea service.

"They're murderers." Matt accepted the cup of tea Narada handed him. The domesticity of the scene as they talked of his parents' murderers was jarring.

"Of your parents," Narada agreed. "And others."

"What others?" Paul asked.

"Several others," Narada answered.

"My uncle for one," Jaijo announced fiercely. "My father's brother."

Narada seated himself at the other end of the table, near where his son stood. He placed his hands together, the palms pressed flush. Old pain and hurt clouded his eyes.

"When?" Matt asked.

"Years ago, back in India," Narada said.

"You know Creighdor killed him?"

The man nodded. "I was there. I saw Creighdor shoot my brother." He ran his fingers through his hair, revealing a long, jagged scar along his right temple. "He shot me after that. I still carry a ball from that confrontation." He tapped his chest near his heart. "Here. Creighdor thought I was dead as well. I wasn't. One ball creased my skull and rendered me unconscious. The other lodged in my chest."

"What happened?" Paul asked.

"My brother had an object that Creighdor wanted." Narada blew on his tea. "My brother had his failings. He had a trace of greed in him. We had come across a piece, an old Egyptian canopic jar, with an interesting history. Do you know what a canopic jar is?"

Matt nodded. "One of the four jars the Egyptians used to store the liver, lungs, and other organs of the dead they mummified." The whole idea, once he'd learned of it, had alternately fascinated him and sickened him. The Egyptians pulled the brain out through the dead person's nose with hooked instruments.

"Yes. The Egyptians knew they had to take those organs out to prevent rot if they wanted to purify and mummify the body of the dead. This particular canopic jar was one of such a set."

"From a single mummy?" Paul asked.

"Yes."

"Who was 'e?" Gabriel asked.

Narada cleaned his glasses absently. "My brother and I hadn't identified the mummy it was from. But Creighdor had. He approached my brother and offered more than our current buyer had offered for the piece. For myself, once I have a piece spoken for, nothing will keep me from completing that transaction. In fact, I make it a practice never to speak of having had a particular piece—if it is a unique item or one that is profitable—even after it is delivered to its new owner."

"Why?" Matt asked.

"Because," Gabriel answered, "if some bloke wants that piece an' can't get it from the seller, why 'e can up an' steal it from the buyer. If 'e knows who the buyer is. An' because them pieces can be stole from them what 'as 'em, knowin' they'll be payin' to get 'em back."

"Yes, that's it exactly." Narada nodded. "This time, though, my brother was tempted. Not only did he admit to owning the piece, but he allowed Creighdor to examine it."

Matt listened attentively, seeing the raw pain etched in Narada's face.

"Letting Creighdor see the jar was a mistake. After he confirmed that it was one he was looking for, Creighdor wouldn't allow my brother to finish his transaction. He demanded that we sell it to him. He kept offering more and more money." Narada stopped for a moment and took a deep shuddering breath. "I arrived after the argument got heated. My brother had held out, telling Creighdor he would have to talk to me." He swallowed. "We talked. I said we could not go back on the deal we had in place. We had our reputations. I even offered to contact the buyer we had and let him know that another collector was making a bid that would triple or quadruple his investment in a matter of minutes."

"That wasn't enough for Creighdor?"

"No. He and his minions pulled out pistols and shot us." Narada sipped his tea, looking like he was talking about the weather instead of such a tragedy. "They took the canopic jar."

"I'm sorry to hear about your loss," Matt said.

Narada nodded. "As I am for yours."

"What was so special about the canopic jar?" Paul asked.

"At that time I did not know. Now I have come to realize that the canopic jar was one of the four that belonged to the mummy at the Fabulous Harn Museum."

Paul leaned forward and unconsciously twisted his walking stick in his hands. "Creighdor tracked down the various pieces of that mummy? Of Pasebakhaenniut?"

"What do you know of Pasebakhaenniut?" Narada asked.

"Only that he was an architect during King Ramses' rule."

"Who told you this?"

"Wentworth," Matt answered. "The museum curator."

Narada let out a breath. "Wentworth is still new to his passion. Perhaps he knows Pasebakhaenniut's corpse, but obviously he doesn't know the story behind the mummy."

"This mummy was different," Matt said. "Wentworth did mention that. Usually only royalty gets buried in a pyramid, but Pasebakhaenniut was buried near the pharaoh's tomb."

"Yes. That's exactly right. Pasebakhaenniut

was one of Ramses' greatest architects. His burial in a tomb of his own was indicative of his importance to the pharaoh."

"Important or not," Paul said, "the man is obviously dead. What difference does it matter if all his pieces are scattered?"

Narada stroked his chin and shook his head. "I don't know. But I do know that your father searched for them as well."

"Other mummies can be purchased with canopic jars that contain the original owner's organs," Paul pointed out. "Surely Creighdor wasn't just a collector looking to complete his collection. He could have bought other mummies if that was what he wanted. In fact, he bought at least one other mummy that we know of. And I certainly know Lord Brockton had no interest in collecting such things."

"Creighdor purchased another mummy?" Narada looked surprised. "When?"

"Two nights ago a ship called *Saucy Lass* put in to harbor carrying a delivery for Creighdor," Matt said. "It looked like a body. We talked with the ship's captain only a short time ago. He confirmed that the cargo was a mummy."

"Interesting." Narada leaned back in his chair and sipped his tea. "Do you know anything about this other mummy?"

"No."

"Why would Creighdor want an additional mummy?" Paul asked.

"For all you know," Gabriel said, "'e's got dozens of 'em back at 'is place. All sittin' to table for tea."

Paul looked irritated. "And the question would still be what Creighdor wants with all of them."

"Let's concern ourselves with the one at the Fabulous Harn Museum for the moment," Matt said.

"Why that one?" Jaijo asked. He stood with his arms crossed and looked indignant.

"Because we know about that one," Matt said. "At least we know something about it. We know that Creighdor is interested in that mummy. We know my father was interested in it. If we can determine what that interest was, perhaps we will know what Creighdor's other mummies, whatever their number, may have in common."

Narada smiled a little and offered Matt a small salute. "Very clear thinking, Lord Brockton."

"Thinking about survival tends to sharpen the mind." *And hope for revenge focuses the thinking.* But he didn't say that aloud.

"As I said," Narada went on, "Pasebakhaenniut was a noted architect for the pharaoh. I got that from the histories my brother and I were able to uncover. But there was more. Pasebakhaenniut was not a native Egyptian. He was from somewhere else."

"There was some mixing of cultures even back then," Paul said, "so the fact that Pasebakhaenniut was from another country is not terribly surprising. Ships had been built that crisscrossed the seas of the known world."

"Yes. And in the Egyptian histories, those other cultures and peoples are acknowledged, either by their own names for their countries or by Egyptian references. However, Pasebakhaenniut is referred to only as one of the 'Outsiders.'"

"Outsiders?" Instantly, Matt felt intrigued.

"A few people who lived at the pharaoh's court were referred to as 'Outsiders.' The Egyptians created a new symbol in their language, or came to use one that became synonymous with the Outsiders until it was no longer used for anything else. The Egyptian people called them that because that was the only information they had about these people. They simply came from . . . *outside*."

"Outside of what?" Paul asked.

"Outside of Egypt, one must suppose."

"With no mention made of where they came from?"

"Not that I've ever read or heard about." Narada cleared his throat. "Everything I've read—Egyptian research papers, translations, and original records—suggest that the Outsiders came from someplace outside Egypt, but there is no indication of how far. According to my own interpretations, they came from an unbelievable distance."

Matt listened attentively.

"The Outsiders," Narada continued, "were a race of people who came into Egypt and became advisers to the pharaohs. According to the records, the Outsiders helped design several of the structures the Egyptians invested so much time, slaves, and resources to make."

"You're suggesting the Sphinx was created by the Outsiders?" Paul asked.

"Perhaps not created," Narada corrected. "But the Outsiders definitely influenced the building of such things. There is even some supposition that they were the first to instruct the Egyptians on how to mummify their dead."

"Why would that skill be necessary?"

"I don't know, but it became so ingrained into the society that it became a cornerstone of Egyptian religion. The few other scholars and relic hunters whom I've talked to over the years think perhaps mummification was originally a religious practice of the Outsiders."

"There are some South American tribes who ascribe to mummification as well," Paul said. "I've talked with ships' captains who have traveled there. And there is the bizarre practice of shrinking the head of a vanquished enemy in Africa."

"According to the legends I've read," Narada said, "the Outsiders may have traveled broadly. Some of the Mayans in Mexico have a greater understanding of mathematics and science than many researchers would have thought possible.

Mummification was also practiced in some of those regions."

"Why would my father have an interest in a mummy even with a background as strange as that?" Matt asked.

Narada shook his head. "Your father wasn't just interested in the mummy, Lord Brockton. He was also interested in the history of the Outsiders. He kept what he'd pieced together of that history in a journal."

"You told him what you told us?"

"Yes. But I think his interest was primarily there because of Lucius Creighdor. It was evident from meeting your father that he knew more about Creighdor's affairs than I did."

"Has Creighdor ever been into your shop?" Paul asked.

"No. He might not even know I have relocated here. He's a man with an immense ego. He might not even remember that he murdered my brother all those years ago and left me for dead."

"It can't have been that long ago," Matt said. "I'm told Creighdor is only twenty-five or twenty-six. I saw him myself only a short time ago. He can't be any older than that."

"My brother was killed seventeen years ago," Narada said. "The man calling himself Lucius Creighdor is much older than he looks."

Matt took that in. That was one discrepancy he hadn't noted. If Creighdor had been responsible for his mother's death seven years ago, he would have been around Matt's age at the time. That didn't make sense either.

"What do you mean, 'calling himself Lucius Creighdor'?" Paul asked.

"That's the name he wears now," Narada said. "Back in India, I knew him as Caspar Denholm. There are others aware of the Outsiders who say Creighdor—and I shall use the name he currently employs so that we may better keep track of him—is well over a hundred years old."

Matt's immediate impulse was to disbelieve the man. "No one lives to be that old."

"Are you calling my father a liar?" Jaijo started forward. He doubled his hands into fists.

Gabriel stepped forward to intercept the other young man.

"No," Matt said, intending the response both as an answer and as a command.

Thankfully, Jaijo and Gabriel came to a halt with little more than an arm's length between them. They gave each other hard, measured looks.

"I'm not questioning your integrity," Matt said to Narada, "but I do question the validity of the rumors."

"As do I," Narada agreed. "However, I have seen Creighdor. He is Denholm. And he looks like a young man in his prime these days, the same as he did seventeen years ago."

"Then we'll have to find a proper answer to

resolve these inconsistencies." Matt thought furiously but couldn't come up with a solution. "You said the Outsiders instructed the Egyptians."

"Yes. They gave them some technology and an understanding of the sciences. According to academicians, there are some . . . gaps, for lack of a better word, that fail to show properly how the Egyptians—and the Mayans and Aztecs, for that matter—achieved the understanding they had at the peaks of their civilizations. A few scholars who are willing to risk their standings in their respective universities believe that the Outsiders guided those peoples in their understanding and knowledge."

"Why?"

"No one knows."

"For their own good," Gabriel said. "You can bet on that. Nobody gives somethin' for nothin', guv'nor. You can take any wager you want on that."

"There is another question." Paul looked at Narada. "Where did these Outsiders go?"

"Some scholars," Narada replied, "believe that the Outsiders died out. Legend has it that they were prone to disease. Contacting new cultures exposed them to several new diseases. And there is another theory that the Outsiders were assimilated by the various cultures, in effect becoming part of the new communities they chose. Such as Pasebakhaenniut the Architect."

"But the technology," Matt said, "did you

ever hear anything about the Outsiders using automatons?"

"They had devices. Egyptian pictographs show several miraculous events. If you interpret the pictographs in a certain fashion. But there is no way of knowing for certain."

In terse sentences stripped of emotion, Matt detailed his encounters with the gargoyles and probable link to the control box he had shot. He didn't know if Narada would believe him.

The man looked amazed. "I've never heard of anything like that."

"I saw it," Matt insisted. "Creighdor has technology like that."

"Perhaps that's the answer," Paul said. "Perhaps Creighdor seeks Outsider technology."

"But the kind of thing Lord Brockton just described didn't exist in anything I've read about," Narada said.

"Them stories an' legends an' the like," Gabriel said, "maybe they didn't tell all of it. Maybe them men what wrote them tales, maybe they didn't know all of it."

"And perhaps the Outsiders disappeared within the cultures they visited," Paul said, "but they still exist today, choosing to remain anonymous, learning and improving the technology they have."

"Creighdor may be looking for these hidden people," Matt said.

"Others have before him," Narada said. "I've

sought them as well. I have several books that I have assembled on the Outsiders if you'd care to have a look."

"Yes. I'd like that very much," Matt responded eagerly. "There is something else that comes to mind. What if this new mummy Creighdor acquired doesn't have anything special about it? What if he intends to use it for another purpose?"

"What purpose?" Narada asked.

"To take the place of the Pasebakhaenniut's mummy in the Fabulous Harn Museum," Matt said.

Gabriel was the first to understand what he was talking about. The young thief grinned from ear to ear. "You think Creighdor means to swap 'em out."

Matt nodded. "It's doubtful that the museum staff would notice. Putting another mummy in the place of the stolen one would prevent the theft reaching the news."

"Creighdor could simply have someone steal the museum's mummy," Jaijo pointed out. "Scotland Yard has enough troubles. The theft of a mummy wouldn't draw much of their attention."

"No, but it might draw the attention of other people who are watching Creighdor," Matt said. "Creighdor may have more enemies than just those in this room."

"I would think so," Narada said. "Those who

survived his wrath or are at cross-purposes with him, of course."

"I have a feeling that those enemies are out there. We just have to find them." Matt stood. "Would you be able to tell one mummy from another?"

Narada stood as well. "Possibly. I've never before had the opportunity to inspect the mummy of an Outsider, but I'd venture that its nature would make itself known in some fashion."

Matt's mind raced. "Then, if you don't mind risking your freedom—and possibly your life—I'd like you to accompany me tonight."

Paul looked uncomfortable and suspicious. "Where?"

"Breakin' into the Fabulous Harn Museum?" Gabriel asked, shaking his head as he realized what Matt planned. "Takin' a peek at that sleepin' corpse all nestled tight in its bandages? You're riskin' a curse."

"I don't believe in curses," Matt said. "I need you to help me, Gabriel. I can't break into that building as easily as you can. But I'll go without you if I have to."

Sourly Gabriel said, "I can't let you do that. I *won't* let you do that."

Matt nodded. "Thank you for that. Maybe we can find out why Lucius Creighdor is so interested in that mummy if we examine it for ourselves." He glanced at Narada. "Are you up to the task? I don't know any other experts in Egyptology."

"I'm hardly an expert," Narada protested.

"You'll know more than I will."

Paul shook his head and tapped his walking stick nervously. "You do realize the courts are still quite fond of hanging thieves, don't you?"

"Only if you're caught." Gabriel smiled. "I'm thinkin' we should plan on *not* gettin' caught. Prolly work out much better for us that way."

"You don't have to go, Paul," Matt said.

His friend's sour grin told him that event was hardly likely, but Matt knew there would be further discussions regarding the matter.

"I'll 'ave a couple of me lads keep an eye on the museum tonight," Gabriel said, "an' on Donovan as well. We should be safe as 'ouses, we should." He frowned. "Except for maybe a curse or two."

Matt looked at Narada. "I won't know what I'm looking for. Whether for links to the Outsiders or to Egyptology."

"Father," Jaijo said, "this is dangerous, and these people are strangers as well as amateurs. Do you really want to risk your freedom and possibly your life by trusting them?"

Narada was quiet for a moment. He stood and locked eyes with Matt. "The man who calls himself Lucius Creighdor is evil, and his organization is larger than anyone might guess." He let out a long breath. "I cannot idly sit by when there is a chance to expose Creighdor for the evil person he is." He offered his hand to Matt. "I will accompany you, and I will pray that we are watched over."

"Good." Matt took the man's hand. Despite the apprehension he felt at the coming endeavor, he couldn't help feeling anticipation. The course he'd chosen was daring, but he felt his father would have approved.

Chapter 13

O nly a handful of hours later—almost midnight, the witching hour—Matt was on Gabriel's heels as they crept through the dark alley behind the Fabulous Harn Museum. The swelling in his face from his earlier run-in with Creighdor's minions had abated, but much of the pain remained, as he was reminded with every rapid thump of his heart that echoed in his swollen features.

Paul trailed Matt, followed by Narada and Jaijo Chaudhary. They all wore black, but Gabriel had taken care to make them rub street dust onto the fabric so the color wouldn't stand out so cleanly black against the buildings. With the road grit in place, Matt knew they more closely matched the shadow-drenched walls of the alley.

A half-dozen of Gabriel's lads watched their backs from strategic corners and rooftops around the museum. All of the lookouts carried whistles of a higher pitch than a uniformed policeman's or watchman's.

In the dark of the night and against the background of river noises, Matt doubted that anyone could tell the difference between the whistles, but they would hopefully add to any confusion necessary to cover a hasty retreat from the museum.

The night watchman hired to guard the museum was gone by the time they arrived at the building. Gabriel had arranged to buy the man off, a common occurrence around so many businesses.

In the alley Gabriel opened the black bag he carried. Kneeling, he took out a small grappling hook that had been specially padded and was affixed to a length of knotted hemp treated with lampblack so it faded into the night.

The young thief stood, whirled the grappling hook, and made a practiced throw up to the building's roof, where it caught the edge. He climbed the rope effortlessly while Matt secured the end.

At the third floor Gabriel took a glasscutter from the tools tied to his left forearm. He cut a hole in the window, reached in, and opened the window. A moment later he was inside. He waved to Matt.

Matt went up the rope next, followed by the other three. The elder Chaudhary proved surprisingly nimble, climbing with only slightly less speed than Gabriel.

Once all of them were inside the building, Gabriel hauled the rope in, left it hanging and ready, and closed the drapes over the window. He took out a small lantern with a hooded bull's-eye that wouldn't allow much light to show, and handed it to Matt.

Matt guided them through the shelves and tables of antiquities, quickly arriving at the sar-cophagus they'd examined earlier. Together, the five of them shifted the heavy stone lid from the container.

Narada brought his own tools from the pack he had strapped over his back. Most of the items were medical equipment. He took out another small lantern and put it on a nearby table.

"This isn't going to be pleasant," Narada announced as he took up a scalpel and leaned over the wrapped mummy.

No one said anything. They all crowded round the sarcophagus and watched as Narada cut the wraps from the desiccated body. When he was finished, there would be no disguising what he had done.

Minutes passed. The only sound came from the thin rasps of the scalpel and the guttering lantern flame. Gradually the body beneath the bandages came into view. The natron salt used to draw the moisture from the body had also left the nut-brown flesh sucked tight to the bone, with the resiliency of stretched leather.

Narada worked in silence. Once he had the cloth out of the way, he turned his attention to the corpse.

Matt wanted to turn away from the hideous sight, but he forced himself to watch. Learning was important. His father had always told him that, and Roger Hunter had led by example.

The corpse lay with its head tilted slightly to one side, like a person deep in thought. Glass eyes peered out of the hollows sunk back into the bony head. The lips pulled back tight, showing blackening teeth that looked rotted and chalky. Red paint covered the withered skin.

"I don't think this is the same mummy as the museum claimed they had," Narada announced.

"Why?" Matt asked.

Narada pointed at the corpse. "Do you see the red paint covering the body?"

"Yes."

"At the time of the twenty-first dynasty, when some of the best-preserved mummies were made, the bodies were painted. Red for men and yellow for women."

"That leads you to believe that this isn't Pasebakhaenniut?"

"Yes. During Ramses' day, in the nineteenth dynasty, bodies weren't painted. Where the skin is not painted it appears to be discolored, which I will have to investigate further."

Paul cursed and drew away, his pale face withdrawing into the shadows.

"What's wrong with you?" Gabriel demanded.

"I know it can't be," Paul whispered, "but I swear to you I thought I saw that thing draw a breath."

A chill thrilled up Matt's spine. *We're tired. That's all. Just tired. That man is dead and he's not going anywhere.* Still, he watched the corpse intently for any signs of movement. There was something about the fact that the mummy was part of Creighdor's schemes that made anything possible.

Narada wiped sweat from his face as he reached for more tools. "A trick of the mind. Perhaps the shadows. Nothing more. This man hasn't lived for a long time."

"Stiffen up," Gabriel advised with obviously newfound courage. "Ain't nuffink to be scairt of in 'ere. Ain't nuffink what can 'urt you."

"I'm not scared," Paul protested. "Just wary. Captain Stebbins seemed so sure of his belief that mummies carried curses." His voice was hollow in the quiet of the museum.

"I need more light," Narada instructed.

Gabriel took the hooded lantern from Matt and leaned in more closely.

With swift economical movements, Narada snipped the sutures holding the mummy's abdomen together. "The Egyptians nearly always took the organs out from the side. For a time they tried inserting a fluid to dissolve them, but the fluid didn't perform well."

Involuntarily Matt opened his mouth and stopped breathing through his nose as a slight stench eddied out into the general vicinity.

"As a general rule," Narada went on, "the mummy-makers left the heart in place. They believed the heart held the deceased's personality as well as his or her ability to feel emotion and to reason." He pulled on a pair of leather gloves. "Over the years, the mummy-makers learned that the organs other than the heart and the kidneys had to be removed to prevent rot."

Jaijo put on gloves as well. At his father's direction he stood on the opposite side of the sarcophagus and caught the side of the undone incision with his hooked fingers.

Narada pressed against the bottom of the incision with his left hand, opening the centuries-old wound, then reached inside the body with his right hand. The thick, dried-out red flesh of the abdomen rippled with his efforts as he rummaged around inside the corpse.

Paul made retching noises. The hooded lantern in Gabriel's grip started to shake. The young thief coughed and gagged.

Marshaling his own self-control, Matt stepped up and took the hooded lantern from Gabriel. Breathing shallowly and scarcely maintaining control, Matt watched in disbelief as Narada delivered what looked like a huge rock from the mummy's stomach.

Narada held up his prize in one hand. The hunk gleamed dully, looking like a huge piece of amber. "In my estimation, this mummy is from the end of the twenty-first dynasty."

"Why?" Matt asked in a strained voice.

"Because the mummy-makers started getting cheap in their preparation of mummies." Narada surveyed the rock. "Instead of packing the stomach cavity with resin-coated linen as they were supposed to, mummy-makers of the late twenty-first dynasty often poured molten resin into the body to occupy space and make it look more lifelike."

"Filling a mold," Matt whispered.

Narada nodded. "More or less. After seeing the mummy's dark discoloration, I guessed that I would find this. Mummy's prepared the old way didn't discolor." He placed the resin aside and let go of the mummy. He leaned on the sarcophagus and peered down at the corpse. "The preservation of the dead wasn't completed nearly as well with this technique, so the flesh turned dark. As this man's did."

"Then this ain't Pasebakhaenniut?" Gabriel asked.

"No."

"So Creighdor an' his people already got the mummy what was in 'ere," Gabriel said. "That's what Donovan was settin' up yesterday when 'e spent all that time here."

"You missed the theft," Paul said.

"I was tailin' a Scotland Yard inspector yesterday," Gabriel retorted. "Not watchin' over a museum. An' you can bet that 'e didn't lift the dead man 'imself. 'E 'ired others what done it."

Matt surveyed the corpse. "Is there any way of knowing who this person was?"

Narada shook his head helplessly. "I have no way of finding out from what you see here. Perhaps Creighdor knows."

Turning away from the body, Matt said, "But we don't know where Creighdor is." He sorted his thoughts quickly, looking for something he could use, some strategy he'd overlooked in the rush of the last couple of days. A thought grazed his mind and he reached out for it. He turned back to the stone sarcophagus. "Creighdor has gone to a lot of trouble to ensure that his theft of the Pasebakhaenniut's mummy escaped detection."

"Yes." Paul moved closer, holding a scented handkerchief over his mouth and nose.

"He used *Saucy Lass* to transport this mummy into the city so he could escape notice," Matt said. "Transporting a mummy through the streets of London would be hard."

"Especially when 'e knows you're up an' lookin' for 'im an' maybe that mummy too," Gabriel said, showing a wolf's grin. "If'n I was tryin' to slip somethin' out of the city that I didn't want just any bloke to know about, why I'd make certain I 'ad a way of transportin' it that I controlled completely an' what wasn't open to too many pryin' eyes."

"You're talking about his ship as well as his carriage," Jaijo said. Interest flickered in his dark eyes.

"Exactly," Matt said, feeling more certain of the logic now that the others saw it as well. "Now that Creighdor has managed to effect the swap, all he has to do is get out of London and deliver Pasebakhaenniut's mummy to a coastal town where he could have a transport group ready."

"If he hasn't done that already," Narada said.

"I don't think so. Business like this, like the delivery two nights ago that my father and I saw, it's better done under the cover of night." Matt blew out his breath. "*Saucy Lass* is still in the docks. Stebbins told us that today."

"Not just in the docks," Gabriel said. "That ship, she's done up at a repair shop Creighdor owns."

Paul tapped his walking stick on the floor. "Chessmore's Shipyards. Creighdor doesn't own the shipyards outright, but he owns a majority."

Gabriel nodded. "That's right. Chessmore's."

"How do you know the ship is there?" Paul asked.

Shrugging, Gabriel said, "Matt mentioned it that night. I know Creighdor's a slippery eel, 'e is. An' when you're watchin' men like 'isself, why you got to watch ever'one round 'im, too. I been lookin' for Scanlon, too, but he's near to vanished. That ship, it was too much a part of this not to keep a lookout on."

Matt took out his pocket watch and turned it so he could see the time in the light from the lantern. "It's a quarter after one." The time surprised him; he wouldn't have guessed they'd been inside the museum that long. He looked up at his companions. "I couldn't think of a better time to have a look at that ship."

"Couldn't be more'n a couple watchmen out there," Gabriel said. "An' there's a quiet way in most don't know about."

Matt paced, feeling the rising excitement flood his body and wash away the fatigue. "Quiet or not, if the ship is still there this venture is going to be dangerous."

"We could wait," Paul suggested.

"For what?" Gabriel demanded. "To 'ave a look at a ship?" He snorted derisively.

"Creighdor's men have already tried to kill us," Paul stated. He pointed the walking stick at the mummy. "When news of this mummy's desecration gets out, who do you suppose he's going to believe was behind it?"

"All the more reason to go now," Matt said, looking at Paul, then taking in the Chaudharys and Gabriel. He knew the young thief would go. Gabriel was always ready for a bit of mischief. "*Saucy Lass* might have sailed during the time we've been here. If she hasn't, the ship will likely sail before dawn. Whatever secrets the mummy has that Creighdor desires and is protecting will disappear."

Paul hesitated. "All right. I'm in." He took a deep breath and looked at Matt. "But it would be better if we didn't go about it as unprotected as babes in the woods."

"We won't," Matt promised. "So far Creighdor has come after us. This time we'll be going after him. Or at least we'll be going after one of his possessions. I don't intend to walk away empty-handed."

A cool wind crossed the Thames and blew through the shipyards at Blackwall Point near the Isle of Dogs. East Indiamen ships were constructed there to sail to the Orient and compete for the spice trade. Fog covered the riverbanks on both sides and masked the lanterns that marked ships and night watchmen. The fog's density restricted Matt's vision as he lay atop a warehouse in back of Chessmore's Shipyards. Patches of it drifted across his line of sight and caused entire ships to disappear till those low-lying clouds passed.

Saucy Lass still occupied a berth inside the shipyards, and Matt felt certain the fog was partly the cause. Getting a ship, even a smaller one like *Saucy Lass*, out into the river and navigating safely through the channel in the night without hitting other ships would have required more luck than skill.

The ship sat tied up inside a construction building that stood 120 feet tall. Most shipyards still built vessels in dry or wet docks under the open sky, but a few of the more modern ship-builders used enclosed spaces like the one Matt studied. Winches, block-and-tackles, and lines were used to set the huge masts in a fraction of the time taken by crews working the riverbanks.

Now, however, Creighdor used Chessmore's Shipyards to hide and protect *Saucy Lass*.

"How many watchmen do you count?" Paul lay on the rooftop beside Matt. His quiet voice didn't carry far.

"Four outside the building," Matt whispered. "But there are others inside." He'd marked the lantern light inside the structure that had drifted by in regular patterns.

"Three inside," Gabriel said.

Agitated, Paul looked at the young thief. "You can see through buildings?"

"No," Gabriel said. "But I can count the number of steps hit takes for a man to walk the length of that building. An' I know 'ow long hit takes for a man to walk them steps for a lantern to go by." He pointed his chin at the building. "There's at least three guards walking a circle inside. Maybe more."

"Even with the sewer access you say the

warehouse has," Paul said, "avoiding three men in the darkness—"

"Possibly more," Jaijo said.

"—will be dangerous."

"We're just going to take a look." Matt collapsed the spyglass he used to watch over the warehouse.

Quietly Matt led the group back down the fire escapes to the alley. On the ground Gabriel once more took the lead, guiding them to a large iron sewer grate at the end of the alley.

Using a hook he produced from the leather bag slung over his back, Gabriel removed the sewer lid. The stench coiled out into the alley like a live thing.

Paul recoiled from the stink. He took a dark blue handkerchief from his pocket and wound it round his face, covering his mouth and nose.

"Powerful bad down there," Gabriel said, "if'n you ain't used to it. I've 'ad lads new to the sewers pass out on me. 'Ad to carry 'em out, I did." He stepped down into the sewer. "Ain't but a short trip to the shipyards. Just keep your mind fixed on that."

Once Gabriel disappeared down into the hole, Matt and the Chaudharys followed, climbing easily down the rungs of the iron ladder mounted on the side.

Paul came last, managing to lever the sewer lid back into place.

The gurgle of running water echoed throughout the sewer. In the darkness, Matt couldn't tell how wide it was. It seemed the sewer ran in a channel between stone shelves that formed walkways. Moving forward, he found the edge of the walkway with his boot, stopping just short of plunging over the side.

"Stop where you are," Gabriel advised. "Water's deep an' carries sickness."

A lucifer flared, lifting Gabriel's face and hands out of the darkness and lending them a wicked orange cast. He touched the match to the wick of a small lantern, got the flame going, and slid the glass back into place.

Looking around the group, Matt saw that his four companions—except for Paul, whose features were covered by the handkerchief—wore grim expressions. No one spoke.

Gabriel took the lead. The lantern light gleamed against the moisture-covered walls. The channel was so wide that Matt knew he couldn't have leapt the distance without a running start. The turgid water eddied and slapped at the sides of the channel as the current ran toward the river.

Ahead, fierce red eyes retreated from the encroaching light. Shrill squeaks echoed down the long tunnel. A moment later some of the rats abandoned their perches on the channel's sides and plopped into the water. The fat bodies floated easily and the black fur turned slick as the long tails dragged through the water.

Matt crept after Gabriel, staying just within the light. Behind him Narada Chaudhary lit a second small lantern. Only the gurgling of the water and the squeaks of the rats interrupted the slap of their feet against the stone.

Chapter 14

Minutes later, Gabriel halted and peered around. Matt came to a stop behind the young thief and gazed at the four-way intersection before them.

"It's awful easy to get lost 'ere," Gabriel whispered. He pushed the lantern in all directions, then looked up. "Most times I don't venture 'ere at all unless I got me a map."

Matt stared along the three other tunnels. Although his nose had become deadened to the stink of the sewer, the air still felt thick and moved reluctantly in and out his lungs.

"This way." Gabriel gripped the lantern's wire handle in his teeth, then jumped up and caught the lip of the cross-tunnel. He worked his way hand over hand to the other side and dropped to the stone. He pointed the lantern's light at the lip. "C'mon then. We ain't got all night."

Matt swung across next, followed by the others. Then Gabriel was off once more.

Only a few feet further on, Gabriel paused again, then darted to the right, following a narrow channel that ran for nearly fifty feet. When he stopped, he looked up.

"That's it, then," Gabriel said as the others joined him. "That's the openin' what leads inside the buildin' where *Saucy Lass* is."

"The sewer opens into a rear room?" Matt asked.

"Yes. Got parts an' tools back there. Bolts of sailcloth. Nails. Barrels an' crates."

Matt grabbed the rungs and started up. Fear pounded inside him. The Webley .455 revolvers he carried weighed his coat pockets down. Gabriel had known a man who had access to a generous supply of firearms. All of them carried weapons.

At the top of the climb, Matt took a deep breath to fill his lungs and clear his mind, then he levered the sewer lid out of the way as quietly as he could. The iron grated against the stone floor, but the sound didn't carry far.

Voices reached Matt's ears at once. He froze, listening, half expecting the men to come investigate the slight noise he'd made. Instead they talked about pubs and past events, and they griped about having to stay up all night guarding the ship.

"—cursed thing makes me skin crawl, it

does," one man groused. "I keep thinkin' maybe I should poke it with me knife an' make sure it ain't just layin' there waitin' on me to turn me back."

"Creighdor don't want that mummy messed with," another man said. "Like as not if'n you damage that bloody thing, Creighdor will have the hide off'n your back, 'e will."

The talk continued as Matt lifted himself out of the sewer into the warehouse supply room Gabriel had told them about. The original building had expanded and covered the sewer in years past. The supply room was a shell, four walls enclosed inside the warehouse. There was no real ceiling. Matt looked up into the shadow-drenched beams of the roof over a hundred feet above.

Below, Gabriel doused the lantern and Narada followed suit. Despite the loss of the light, a small window set high into the wall allowed enough moonlight in that Matt could see his way around the spare parts, barrels, and bolts of sailcloth that littered the room.

"The rafters." Gabriel pointed up.

Above the wall, only the open rafters formed a kind of open ceiling over the storeroom.

"We can climb up," Gabriel whispered, pointing to the long ladder built into a nearby wall. "Get a better look at things." He moved a barrel against the wall, clambered on top, and caught the top of the room's wall. He hauled himself up onto the nearest rafter, then edged over to the long ladder.

Matt followed. The ladder was stout oak, built to last, and he reached the upper rafters in short order. With higher beams above to hold on to, he had no problem standing and walking along the rafters. They definitely had the high ground.

Below their position, *Saucy Lass* sat in the middle of the open space in the building's main work area. Thick hawser ropes tied to pilings standing up from the wet dock kept the ship from banging against the wooden walkways surrounding her. Furled sails filled the yardarms. Rigging running from the masts to the ship's deck looked like spiderwebs.

Riding the river current, *Saucy Lass* tested her restraints. Timbers groaned and creaked as the ship bobbed, and rigging rattled against the 'yards.

Four night watchmen circled the ship, crossing over the catwalk above the huge double doors that ended only inches above the river surface. They continued talking, never guessing that Matt and his companions hung a hundred feet over their heads.

Matt watched the ship carefully to see if there were any watchmen aboard *Saucy Lass* as well. After long moments of listening to the blood pump through his ears, he looked at Gabriel.

The young thief shook his head.

"I'm going to have a look aboard," Matt whispered. He reached for a coil of rope attached to one of the beams over the ship. The ropes were used to raise and lower tools and to brace one-hundred-foot masts that were being replaced on ships in for repairs.

"No." Paul caught Matt's arm. "You can't go down there."

The river lapping at the ship and the noise filtering in from other vessels and crews out on the water kept the men below from hearing them.

Matt looked at his friend. "There's no other way. We need to know if the mummy is aboard. *I* need to know, Paul. My father died for a reason."

Slowly, Paul released his hold. "Be careful."

Matt nodded. He let the rope down slowly, trusting the shadows that filled the center of the huge warehouse to keep him masked. When the watchmen continued their rounds none the wiser, Matt slid down the rope just as slowly. The rough hemp rasped against the leather gloves he wore.

No sooner had he reached the ship's deck than Matt became aware that the rope shuddered in his grasp. He looked up, then moved away just in time to avoid Gabriel's boots as he slid down the rope as well.

"Can't let you come down 'ere all by yerself, Matt," Gabriel said with a crooked grin.

"Two of us can get trapped easier than one," Matt said, ducking down as one of the watchmen turned around suddenly to talk to another man.

"Maybe. But one can't watch over 'is own backside while 'e's lookin' forward, can 'e?"

Lantern light skated across the deck. Shadows scurried away for a moment, then returned. The men carried on a spirited conversation filled with ribald tales.

Staying low, Matt made his way to the center cargo hold. The captain's quarters on the ketch was a small, cramped affair. He knew the mummy, if it were aboard the ship, wouldn't be kept there.

Thankfully the cargo hold was open. Matt went down the ladder to the waist deck. Below, he drew one of the large Webley revolvers Gabriel had negotiated for. The large-caliber weapon had a lot of knockdown power, but it was also a visible threat that would give a man instant pause.

Gabriel drew a revolver as well. They split up, Matt going forward and Gabriel going to the stern. After a quick inspection, they discovered that the rooms in the waist were empty of crew as well as the mummy.

Peering down into the main hold, Matt saw a lantern burning that provided enough light to see the long ladder that led down into the cargo space. Stone ballast occupied the bottom of the ship's hold, keeping *Saucy Lass* bottom-heavy so she could ride out rough seas. Several crates and barrels filled the hold as well, most of them provisions and cargo left over from Stebbins's run to Egypt.

A stone sarcophagus sat in the stern of the

ship. The lantern light poured molten orange over the rough stone surface.

"Well," Gabriel whispered, "looks like we got the box the corpse back at the Fabulous Harn Museum come in. Guess we ought to take a look an' find out if the missin' mummy done got 'isself a new 'ome."

Matt clambered down the ladder to the floor of the main cargo hold. He kept the pistol ready in his fist. Images of the night *Saucy Lass* arrived ricocheted in his thoughts.

My father died for the secret in that box, he thought. He felt the heaviness of the mysterious iron key lying hard against his chest over his beating heart as he strode across the flat planking above the stone ballast. *At least that was* one *of the secrets he died for.*

Matt's boots thudded against the planks and echoed in the cavernous space of the cargo hold. He ignored the sound, focused entirely on the sarcophagus. He remembered Stebbins's talk at the pub of how he and the crew had feared the cargo of death they had carried. Fear thrilled inside him as well as he gripped the sides of the stone lid.

With Gabriel's help, he managed to lever the sarcophagus lid to one side. Shadows covered the figure inside.

Matt crossed to the lantern hanging on the wall and brought it back to the sarcophagus. He shined the light on the bandage-wrapped corpse of a man who had died thousands of years ago.

"Do you think it's the one?" Gabriel asked.

"It has to be," Matt answered. "Why would Creighdor go to all the trouble of switching mummies simply to end up with the wrong one?"

"So what's so special about it?"

Matt moved the lantern light more slowly. He wasn't certain if Narada Chaudhary would know.

Light caught in the glass eyes and glowed pale green. The color was so strong that Matt could have sworn it came from inside the mummy. He leaned down, moving the lantern closer and staring into the dead man's eyes.

The pale green glow persisted.

Matt reached for the eyes.

"Don't," Gabriel warned. He produced a knife with a long, thin blade. "For all you know, it's poisoned."

Matt drew his hand back. "I hadn't thought of that."

"This 'ere mummy," Gabriel said, thrusting the point of the knife under the left glass eye, "it could be a trap, it could. Don't know why else Creighdor would leave it layin' about all lit up like this."

Breathing shallowly, focused on Gabriel's actions, Matt watched as the knifepoint lifted the glass eye free. Behind the glass eye, the pale green glow burned like liquid fire.

"What's causin' that?" Gabriel asked in a hushed voice.

"I don't know." Matt pulled the lantern back.

The pale green light seemed to glow more brightly. "Something's inside the head. Let me borrow your knife."

Gabriel handed the blade over.

Hypnotized by the mystery rather than the horrid act he was about to perform, Matt slid the blade toward the eye socket filled with green fire. As soon as the blade touched the glow, sparks jumped, flaring like Chinese fireworks.

An invisible fist smashed into Matt's chest, knocking him backward several feet. Paralyzed, his breath stayed locked in his throat and he couldn't feel his heart beat.

"Matt!" Gabriel hissed, rushing over. Panic filled his face as he knelt down at Matt's side. "Matt!"

In the next instant, just as Matt's vision started to pulse and turn black around the edges, the band of force around his chest relaxed and went away. He let out a long breath, then sucked in another one greedily. The paralysis lifted.

"Are you all right?" Gabriel asked worriedly.

"Yes." Gingerly, Matt sat up. He reached out for the knife and picked it up. Upon closer inspection, he saw that the point still glowed cherry red from heat. He pushed himself to his feet and returned to the mummy.

The pool of pale green remained undisturbed in the eye socket.

"That was some kind of power," Matt said aloud. "I felt it slam into me."

Gabriel grabbed his arm. "Quiet." He looked up and cocked an ear.

Matt listened, hearing the footsteps topside on the deck.

"Somebody's on the ship," Gabriel said.

The footsteps continued, then changed in pitch.

"Comin' down the ladder," Gabriel said. "Whoever it is, 'e's 'eaded this way."

Matt examined the mummy and found the glass eye under the dead man's chin. Quickly, he used a handkerchief to pick the glass eye up and put it back into the eye socket.

Together, he and Gabriel slid the sarcophagus lid back into place. He hung the lantern back where he'd gotten it. Then they hurried to the nearest stack of crates.

Matt hid in the shadows, trying desperately to control his breathing. He reached into his coat pockets and brought out both Webley pistols.

A man carrying a lantern clambered down the ladder into the hold. Lucius Creighdor and five other men followed only a couple of moments later.

"We're in for it now," Gabriel whispered.

"Cool heads," Matt whispered back. He peered around the corner of the crate in front of him. In the shadows they were almost invisible.

Creighdor stopped beside the sarcophagus and gestured impatiently. Two of the men removed the sarcophagus lid. Creighdor took a strange-looking device from his pocket and pressed it to the mummy's head.

Without warning, the mummy sat bolt upright. The arms dangled at its sides lifelessly, but the head tilted back. The glass eyes shot from the mummy's eye sockets and clanked against the wooden plank floor, then rolled away. Green light jetted from the eye sockets and the gaping mouth.

The green glow came to a stop only a foot or two in front of the mummy's face. Gradually the light sharpened, creating three-dimensional images in the air.

Creighdor stepped to the top of the sarcophagus so that he stared over the mummy's shoulder. He spoke, but the language was nothing that Matt recognized.

One of the other men spoke in the same language. That man took out another device and pointed it at the image that projected from the mummy's eyes and mouth. Creighdor spoke softly, short phrases, as if commanding responses.

As Matt watched in disbelief, the images captured in the green glow sharpened still more. With the clearer representation, he saw pyramids and shifting sands, people dressed in strange clothing. Then the images flickered and changed again, becoming a montage of bright spots that Matt figured were stars. A comet burned across the scene. In the next moment, strange symbols twisted into shape in the air.

Creighdor spoke again, still in the strange language that Matt couldn't understand. The other man nodded and spoke in the same tongue.

Blueprints followed the strange symbols. The appearance of the new material obviously piqued Creighdor's interest, because he stepped around the mummy so that he could better observe the design. When Creighdor spoke this time, his voice betrayed excitement.

Abruptly, the mummy's eyes and mouth turned dark. Jerking and twitching, the corpse collapsed back into the sarcophagus.

Creighdor cursed. Some of the words were in English so Matt understood the intent if not the design. Creighdor took the device from his pocket again and shoved it against the mummy's head. The corpse jerked and shivered, but remained in repose within the sarcophagus. Sparks ran the length of the mummy, and it gradually settled back into its lifeless appearance. The eyes and mouth flickered green for a moment, but there was no strong response.

Has it used up all the energy stored inside it? Matt wondered. *Or is it broken?* He wondered at the mummy's nature, thinking perhaps it might be some kind of automaton like the gargoyles. *But with all the organ removal the Egyptians did on the corpse, wouldn't they have noticed if they were preparing an automaton for mummification? Would they have done such a thing?* Questions danced through Matt's head, but he had no answers for any of them. He flexed his hands on the Webleys, taking fresh grips as Creighdor peered around the hold. For a moment Matt believed the man might have somehow sensed him hiding in the shadows.

Then Creighdor spoke to the men standing nearby. "Close it," he commanded. "I will try again later. It still hasn't finished its recovery phase."

The men replaced the stone lid on the sarcophagus. Creighdor walked back to the ladder leading up to the waist of the ship.

Matt waited until he'd heard all of them exit the boat. Then he put away the pistols and approached the sarcophagus.

"Help me," he told Gabriel.

Gabriel grabbed the other end of the lid. "What are you plannin' on doin'?"

"Maybe the Chaudharys will know about what the mummy does. There could be information here we can use against Creighdor." Matt lifted his end of the lid clear and the swung it to the floor. "Evidently Creighdor didn't get everything he wanted from it."

Gabriel looked down at the body. "This . . . this . . . thin'—it 'as to be some kind of machine. It must be some kind of machine."

"I don't know." Matt looked around for the cooper's box he saw earlier. The ship's cooper built barrels to transport oil and spices. The box held a saw. He took the saw out.

"What are you gonna do with that?" Gabriel asked.

"We can't take the whole body when we go." Matt grabbed the mummy's shoulder. "Help me."

"Help you what?"

"Move the body. Slide it backward."

Together, they managed to drag the body out of the sarcophagus till the head protruded over the edge.

"What now?" Gabriel asked.

Without answering, Matt lifted the saw and set the jagged blade at the mummy's throat.

"You're not gonna—"

Matt's first pass with the saw cut deep into the mummy's neck and cut off Gabriel's words. Matt silently gave thanks that there was no blood involved. He kept sawing, throwing himself into the gruesome work. He fought the saw, jerking the blade free each time the teeth got caught in the mummified flesh. Ten more passes and he was up against the spinal column connecting to the skull. Three more passes and even the spine separated.

The head dropped free of the mummy's body and bounced and rolled across the floor. Gabriel jumped out of the way, dodging back quickly as the head rolled with the gentle pitch and swell of the ship riding the river currents.

Matt let go of the saw and went after the head. He'd come this far, risked his life and the lives of his friends, and he was determined not to lose whatever further examination the mummy's head might reveal. He picked the head up in both hands just as one of the men who had been with Creighdor came back down the ladder.

Chapter 15

Shifting the mummy head to the crook of his arm, Matt reached for the Webley pistol in his right coat pocket.

"No, don't," Gabriel said, stepping forward with his right arm drifting back to pick up the lid of a crate.

The man on the ladder reached for the pistol holstered at his hip and opened his mouth to scream. Before he could make a sound, Gabriel whacked the crate lid against his head in a fluid, practiced throw. The man fell from the ladder, dropping heavily to the wooden planks covering the floor of the cargo hold.

"If you'd shot 'im," Gabriel said, "you'd 'ave alerted Creighdor an' them. This way, maybe we got a chance to get out of 'ere before we're discovered." He ran to check on the man, who was lying unconscious in a heap.

Matt took the cooper's apron from the box

and made a sling for the decapitated head, wrapping his grisly burden up tight, then slinging it over his shoulder.

"You ready?" Gabriel asked.

Matt gave his friend a tight nod. As Gabriel went up the ladder with pistol in hand, Matt stopped to take the man's pistol from his holster. His father had taught him never to leave an opponent behind with a weapon that could be used. He thrust the pistol into his pocket and climbed the ladder. His breath burned into his lungs.

They made the waist without getting spotted, then headed for the deck.

Matt was halfway out of the hold when someone called out, "Chauncey, did you get that whiskey out of the 'old?"

Then a lantern beam swung round and pinned Gabriel in its Cyclopean gaze.

"That ain't Chauncey," another watchman said.

Curses swelled into the warehouse, lost in the sudden thunder of gunfire.

Matt scrambled up, watching in horror as Gabriel was hit and spun around. The only stroke of good fortune was that he was knocked out of the glaring lantern's view.

The watchmen ran toward the gangplanks laid to the wooden walkway on the starboard side. Harsh explosions filled the warehouse's interior.

Staying low, Matt swung around and brought his captured pistol to bear. He aimed for the lantern shining across the deck, then squeezed the trigger.

The lantern exploded and the light went away. A man's hoarse scream punctuated the gunfire that raked the ketch's deck, masts, and rigging. Then the lantern's wick caught its hapless bearer on fire as the flame sought out the oil that had splashed across the man's clothing. Flames crawled up the man as he whirled, then jumped into the sea trapped between the walkway and the ship.

"Gabriel!" Matt called, near-to-blinded from the lantern lights shining in his eyes.

"'Ere, Matt." Gabriel moved in the darkness, favoring his left arm but pulling his pistol up in his right hand and firing toward a watchman charging up the gangplank.

The bullet caught the man and hurled him backward.

"You're wounded," Matt said.

"Yes." Gabriel kept firing till his pistol emptied. He knelt down behind the mainmast and broke his weapon open. He fumbled extra cartridges from his pockets and reloaded. "Creighdor didn't get clear. Saw 'im up by the doors."

Despite the situation, Matt couldn't help glancing forward and seeing Creighdor standing near the doors leading out to the river. Matt raised his pistol and fired twice. Both rounds came close to the mark but must have missed. Or if they hit, Creighdor gave no indication. Matt suddenly remembered how his father had shot Josiah Scanlon squarely in the chest to no avail.

Bullets dug splinters from the deck only inches from Matt. The weight of the mummy's head, which felt hard as a rock, slammed into his back as he ran to join Gabriel.

One of the other watchmen along the walkways suddenly twisted and dropped into a heap. Only then did Matt hear the shots that came from above. He glanced up and saw gunfire blasting out of the shadows along the beams almost one hundred and twenty feet above. The distance might as well have been to the moon.

"We've got to get out of here," Matt said, leaning out and firing his three remaining shots with the captured weapon.

"I'm open to suggestion," Gabriel replied gamely. He snapped the cylinder closed on his pistol.

Matt tossed his weapon over the side of the ship and drew one of the Webleys. "Feel like a swim?"

"Can't," Gabriel answered. "I can't move me arm so good." He paused. "You're gonna 'ave to go on without me, Matt."

"No."

"Ain't no sense in both of us dyin' 'ere

tonight. Somebody's gotta carry on the fight. I just got unlucky, is all."

"I'm not leaving without you." Another man tried to make it up the gangplank, but Matt shot him. The man turned and fell over the side, plunging into the water.

"Won't be long before Creighdor calls in them gargoyles. Once they get 'ere, what chance are you gonna have?" Gabriel swallowed and tried to look brave. "You gotta go, Matt."

"No."

"Then you're stupid." Gabriel's tone turned ugly and hard. "You know I don't 'old with spendin' me time with stupid people. They gets on me nerves. An' right now you're gettin' on me nerves. Never expected that of you."

"There have been other times we got into bad trouble," Matt said. "We never ran out on each other then. I'm not going to start now."

Bullets ripped across the deck and tore splinters from the railing and masts. At the front of the building Creighdor opened a side door and rushed outside.

"'E's goin' for reinforcements," Gabriel stated grimly.

"I know." Matt peered around the mast and took deliberate aim on one of the watchmen standing in the warm glow of a lantern he'd only just abandoned. His bullets missed the man twice, but drove him into hiding behind a stack of crates.

"Matt!"

Looking up, Matt tried to find Paul amid the beams over the ship. Instead, a cargo net came plunging out of the shadows and thumped against the ship's deck. A spiderweb of ropes splashed across the deck, spreading in an ever-widening pool.

Muzzle flashes marked Paul and the Chaudharys' positions. Matt was relieved to see that they were skilled and experienced enough to change places after every shot so the surviving watchmen couldn't target their positions.

"Grab onto the net," Paul said. "We'll pull you up. Hurry!"

"We get into that net," Gabriel said, "we ain't gonna be nuffink but a sackful of easy targets."

"It's the only chance we have." Matt took Gabriel by the upper arm and pulled him into motion. The shadows aboard *Saucy Lass* still helped mask them from Creighdor's guards and watchmen.

Evidently Paul and the Chaudharys' marksmanship had chewed through the ranks of Creighdor's men. Matt marked only two positions where the watchmen continued to fire. His companions' fire kept those two tucked back under cover.

The big doors at the front of the building swung open slowly as more men poured in the same way Creighdor had exited. Fog swirled through the doors as Matt grabbed hold of the loose folds of the cargo net. He stepped up into the net so that his legs took nearly all of his weight. Beside him, Gabriel did the same thing.

"They're over there!" one of the two surviving watchmen squalled. "Hangin' on that net!"

Lantern lights converged on the cargo net, followed swiftly by the cracks of firearms and bullets.

"They're never gonna pull us up in time," Gabriel said.

Holding onto the net with one hand, Matt fired his Webley into the center of the knot of men. One of them went down, driven backward by one or more rounds. The rest of the men scattered.

"Hold on tight," Paul called down. "You're going to come up fast. If we lose you, we won't get another chance."

"Ready," Matt called up. He looped one hand through the net and switched his empty pistol for the one that still held rounds.

"Now!" Paul yelled.

Wood rasped overhead. Glancing up, Matt saw one of the timbers that had lain across the beams overhead suddenly fall through the rafters. The falling timber far outweighed Matt and Gabriel, and they shot upward to the rafters. Paul had tied the timber to the other end of the line to use as a counterweight. The falling timber almost collided with them, but the threat was gone in the same instant that Matt recognized it.

Then the cargo net slammed home against the block-and-tackle that supported it. The pulley wheels shrilled as the net choked the device to a stop.

"Climb!" Paul ordered. He sat perched on the rafter only a few feet above.

"Gabriel's hurt," Matt responded.

"I can take care of meself," Gabriel said. "Ain't the first time I've 'ad to climb with a busted wing." He started gamely up the net, using it like a rope ladder.

Paul leaned down and caught the back of Gabriel's coat, adding his strength to the young thief's. "Keep coming then. I've got you."

Lantern lights strobed the darkness collected in the rafters, but the distance proved too much for the beams to provide much help. Still, the guards fired round after round.

Jaijo crawled along the beam and helped Paul pull Gabriel up, then helped the young thief get his footing.

Matt clung to the cargo net, spinning round and round. The fog filled half of the warehouse now, pushing gray vapor into the darkness.

The guards pounded along the wooden walkways, then onto the ship.

"Cut the rope," Creighdor called from the walkway. "Cut the rope and the net will fall."

One of the men sprang toward the rope tied to the timber that had dropped into the water beside the ship. A knife blade splintered the light.

"Climb, Matt," Paul yelled down. "I don't know if the net's jammed into the machinery enough to hold once they cut free the counterweight."

Matt climbed, swiftly gaining the rafter just as the guard's knife sliced through the rope. The timber sank into the dark water and a bullet from Narada Chaudhary's pistol slammed the man to the deck. Matt caught hold of the rafter and heaved himself up.

"What are those?" Jaijo asked in a strangled, hoarse voice.

Following the line of Jaijo's eyes, Matt saw a half-dozen gargoyles through the building's open doors. They looked like heavy-bodied birds as they beat their wings slowly.

"Go!" Matt yelled.

They ran as quickly as they dared along the rafters, heading for the storeroom at the back of the building and the escape route provided by the sewer. Ahead of Matt, Jaijo slipped and almost fell. Matt caught the young man's coat and anchored himself to one of the support beams, barely managing to keep them both on the rafter. Then they were running again.

Matt pulled his loaded pistol from his pocket as he ran. The noise of the gunshots and the yells sounded loud against the building's roof.

The gargoyles flew into the building with little sound. Two of them landed in the ship's rigging and gazed around, searching for prey. Others circled the building's interior.

A gargoyle spotted the five rushing through the rafters and altered its flight path, aiming itself at them.

Matt turned on the rafter and brought up the Webley in both hands. He focused on the horrid, leering face, then squeezed off shot after shot. Two rounds struck sparks from the creature's body. The third shot shattered the gargoyle's features and caused flames to shoot from the hollow head.

The gargoyle went inert and crashed into the rafter. The vibration nearly knocked Matt from his feet. He lunged forward and caught the upright beam ahead of him.

Paul reached the beams over the storeroom and dropped immediately, followed by Gabriel, Narada Chaudhary, and Jaijo. By the time Matt scrambled down the ladder, Paul was already dropping through the manhole.

Creighdor roared curses and orders.

Matt didn't think Creighdor had gotten a good look at him. On the ladder over the storeroom, aware that at least one of the gargoyles and several of the guards were closing in on him, Matt dropped feet first into the storeroom fifteen feet below.

Cruel pain bit into Matt's shoulder and his downward plunge halted without warning. Realizing he was caught by the sling he'd made of the cooper's apron for the severed mummy's head, Matt glanced up frantically.

A gargoyle perched on the storeroom wall

above Matt. Massive clawed feet bit into the wood. Its beak held the sling with the severed head, suspending Matt a few feet above the floor. The gargoyle's features made it resemble some great bird of prey, a hawk perhaps, but of gargantuan size.

The sharp beak opened. Glassy eyes studied Matt dispassionately.

Has it actual thoughts? Matt wondered. *With the intensity it's looking at me, it must.*

But even as he was exploring that possibility, part of his mind was screaming in primitive fear as the gargoyle drew him forward and opened its beak wider.

Matt lifted his pistol. He knew only two or three rounds remained. He hoped it would be enough. He pushed the barrel into the creature's beak and squeezed the trigger. In the enclosed space of the storeroom, the thunder of the gunshot was deafening. Stone splinters flew from the gargoyle's broken head, cutting Matt's face.

As Matt hit the ground, he clung to the wall, just managing to stay out from under the gargoyle as it shattered into a thousand pieces against the storeroom floor. The thing's beak broke as well, freeing its grip on the makeshift sling. The mummy's head landed next to Matt as he drove the breath from his lungs.

"Hunter!" Jaijo called from the manhole.

Stunned for a moment, Matt tried in vain to get to his feet. Above him, another gargoyle swooped over the storeroom, then circled back round. In the next instant, heated green beams lanced through the storeroom door and walls, turning those edifices into Swiss cheese.

Beams set bags of dry goods on fire; speared through casks of wine, releasing spigots of fluid to splatter on the floor; and pierced crates and hogsheads of molasses.

Flailing, Matt turned himself over just as Jaijo caught his ankle and pulled him toward the manhole. During the mad scramble, Matt noticed a group of barrels set apart from the others. He noted the triple Xs across their fronts and realized they held gunpowder.

He cursed to himself, realizing it was a wonder they hadn't already blown up. The only thing that had probably saved them was the sheets of hammered metal used for barrel-making that sat behind them.

"Let go of my ankle," Matt said.

"They're coming," Jaijo called from the manhole.

Matt knew. His peripheral vision told him that more gargoyles clustered overhead like a flock of carrion birds. One of them swooped down and landed inside the storeroom. The massive wingspread hindered the creature, trapping it for just an instant.

Pushing himself to his feet, Matt reached the small gunpowder kegs. He used his pistol to stave in the top of one of them, then threw a trail of black powder out, making certain the powder trail was unbroken so that it led back to the broken keg and the other containers.

Bullets struck the hammered metal, vibrating them against the wall.

Matt broke his empty pistol open and plucked two spare cartridges as the gargoyle lumbered toward him. The creature brushed shelves aside as if they were nothing. But the falling shelves created a blockade in front of the gargoyle, slowing it down.

Holding the two cartridges between his thumb and first two fingers the way his father had trained him to do a rapid reload of a revolver, Matt shoved them into the cylinder. He snapped the pistol closed and pulled the barrel in line with the gargoyle as the creature reached for him.

He squeezed off the first shot at point-blank range. The powerful .455 round cored through the gargoyle's face and blew out the back of its head, scattering the mysterious metal boxes. Sparks jumped as the gargoyle locked up.

Two other gargoyles landed in the storeroom and started for Matt immediately.

Turning back to the line of powder he'd poured, Matt pointed the pistol and pulled the hammer back with his thumb. He held the barrel only inches from the black powder, then pulled the trigger.

The muzzle flash caught the powder on fire. Thick gray smoke poured up and followed the slow-burning powder snaking back to the pile of powder kegs.

Matt turned back to the manhole. Jaijo dropped out of his way just as he stepped into the hole. Matt plummeted into the sewer and landed off-balance. He fell heavily, and pain shot through his left ankle.

"Let's go," Jaijo said, grabbing a double fistful of Matt's coat and yanking him to his feet.

Matt stood and stumbled after Jaijo as they fled through the sewers. The mummy's head banged against his back.

"Run!" Jaijo shouted at the others. "Matt's set fire to the powder kegs!"

Paul held the lit lantern they'd left down in the sewers.

As Matt turned the corner at the end of the small tunnel back into the main one, the gunpowder exploded. A violent whirlwind of force hammered through the tunnel, caught Matt just ahead of a belch of black smoke and fire, and hurled him forward into the dark sewer water. The bright orange flames reflected against the water's surface and the eyes of at least a dozen rats swimming there.

The water was deeper than Matt would have thought. He submerged, panicked for a moment, then touched the bottom of the channel with a foot and pushed back up. He broke the surface, whipped the hair out of his eyes, and tried not to think of the foulness that covered him.

Turning in the chill water, he gazed back along the side tunnel. Light from the storeroom and dock enabled him to see that the manhole was covered with debris. Cracks spiderwebbed the stone floor around it.

Paul and Jaijo returned for him, helping him out of the water. Drenched and chill, hardly able to stand the stink of himself, Matt checked to make certain he hadn't lost the mummy's head.

"They can't follow us down 'ere," Gabriel said. "Even if they find another way down into the sewers, it won't be in time. An' they won't know which way we went."

Matt nodded. Together they headed out of the sewers.

Epilogue

Matt stood out in the swirling fog that lay over Blackwall Point and watched the fire-boats out on the Thames struggling with the blaze that steadily consumed Chessmore's Shipyards.

The explosions and the accompanying fires had drawn sailors and longshoremen from rented rooms, pubs, and other ships sitting at anchor. Groups of them stood nearby and up and down the riverbanks along the Isle of Dogs. All of them speculated about the cause of the explosions.

"Do you see Creighdor?" Matt asked Paul, who stood with a spyglass to his eye.

"No." Paul continued studying the crowds. "Maybe he was caught in the blast."

"Others made it out of there alive," Narada stated quietly. "*We* made it out of there alive. There's no reason to believe that Creighdor was harmed in any way. More than likely he doesn't want to attract a lot of attention. I think he would try to escape notice."

"I'm beginning to think Creighdor's got more lives than a cat," Gabriel said. His wounded arm hung in a makeshift sling under his coat. Luckily the bullet had gone through and wouldn't require extraction. After a few days of rest he'd be good as new, but for the moment he was in a lot of pain.

Matt had dumped his own sodden coat in the nearest trash barrel as soon as they'd climbed out of the sewers. There was nothing he could do about his wet clothes at the moment, however. He smelled rank. None of his companions wanted to stand close to him. He didn't blame them. He could hardly stand to smell himself, and wouldn't have if he'd had a choice. He took the blanket Gabriel had promptly stolen from one of the boats they passed and wrapped it around himself. The warmth made standing there in the wind almost tolerable.

Two of the fireboats rowed hard, pulling at the lines that led into the burning warehouse. Slowly, *Saucy Lass* slid out of her berth inside the building and came out into the river. Flames covered her rigging and sails. The aft mast was broken, leaning over into the foremast, held up only by the rigging. The damage done to the ship was mute testimony to how powerful the blast had been. Other fireboat crews manned pump-fed hoses and tried to extinguish the fires covering the ship's deck. If *Saucy Lass* ever took back to the sea, it would be only after considerable repairs.

The damage to the ship made Matt feel good. His strike against Creighdor tonight had cost the man a shipyard and the mummy's head. As well as whatever secrets it held.

But you haven't paid enough yet, Matt vowed. He swore that upon the lives of his parents.

"Staying in the vicinity of all this might not be a good idea," Jaijo commented. "You've already said Inspector Donovan of Scotland Yard was looking for you, and there's no doubt that Creighdor has other spies open to him. We have no idea where Scanlon is, for one."

Unconsciously, Matt glanced up at the sky. Patchy fog covered the black night sky. No gargoyles were in sight.

"You're right," he told Jaijo. He turned and led the group away, moving between the buildings and the boats anchored on the riverbanks.

"So what do you have in the sling?" Paul asked as he fell into step beside Matt.

During the confusion and the need to attend to Gabriel's wound, no one had asked about the pack Matt had carried up from *Saucy Lass*'s cargo hold. He halted at the nearest alley and quickly unwrapped his gruesome prize.

Paul stepped back. "I don't know which smells worse. You or that foul head."

"Creighdor chopped the head from the mummy?" Narada asked.

"No," Gabriel said, grinning with pride. "Matt did it. Took "isself up a cooper's saw an' sawed the head right off."

"Taking a trophy?" Paul asked.

"Couldn't "ave brought the whole body up, now could we?" Gabriel asked.

"Why would you want to?"

Quickly, Matt explained all that he and Gabriel had seen down in the hold.

"The mummy was communicating?" Narada asked.

"No," Matt answered. "What I saw looked more like . . . like . . ." He sighed. "I don't know what it looked like. But the mummy wasn't talking the way you and I are talking now. It was like a record of something, all made up of moving photographs somehow. I *saw* Egypt. I saw pyramids and people dressed in strange clothing. It had to be Egypt."

Matt tilted the head back. Green light danced in the eye hollows for a moment, then went dark.

"May I?" Narada reached for the head.

"Is it some kind of automaton?" Paul asked, sounding hopeful that they might not be examining the head of a corpse.

"No," Narada said. "This was once flesh and blood. I wish I could have examined the body. If this is Pasebakhaenniut, I should very much have liked to see him. I've never seen the body of an Outsider before. If that is what he was."

The eye hollows flickered green lights again.

"Creighdor wanted that mummy," Matt said. "There's a reason he considered it valuable. We have to figure out what that reason was and find out if we can use that knowledge against him."

"We will." Narada rolled the head over, unconcerned that it had once belonged to a living, breathing person. "If the mummy was able to make those light images, there must be a power source somewhere."

"The lights still flicker in the eyes," Matt said.

"Could be a residual power." Narada turned the head over again and examined the jagged neck stump. The cut had not been clean. The cooper's saw was designed for quickly ripping through boards and planks, and Matt had been in a hurry. "Maybe whatever still lurks in this dead man's head is self-contained." He handed the head back to Matt. "When we get back to my shop, we can investigate. We'll know soon enough."

Matt wrapped the head back in the cooper's apron and slung it over his back. He gazed at the river where the fireboats still struggled with the blazing warehouse.

"Whatever we find out," Gabriel said quietly, "it 'ad better be good. Creighdor, 'e ain't gonna like us much after this. An' 'e might still want that 'ead back."

"That's fine," Matt said. "Let him come." *Let Scanlon come too*, he thought. Both men were going to pay for the murders they'd committed.

They were silent for a moment, then Paul said, "We're not ready for something like this, Matt. Creighdor is too powerful, too . . . *different*. We don't even know who—or what—we're truly facing."

"We'll learn," Matt said. "We're already learning. And tonight we served notice on the hunter. He's one of the hunted as well." He looked at his companions. "If any of you want to back out of this, I'll understand. This was my father's fight, but now I'm making it mine. I will not rest until I see Creighdor dead or exposed for whatever he is."

All of them shook their heads.

"I can't let you do this on your own," Paul said. "Creighdor is too powerful. Your father's note suggested that Creighdor's plans even threaten England. I won't stand by while my country is menaced. And I am your friend." He shoved a hand out between them. "I pledge my loyalty to you in this endeavor, Matt. For as long as you need me and will have me in it with you."

"As do I," Narada said, adding his own hand. "I've hunted the being that calls itself Lucius Creighdor for years. For whatever reason, Lord Brockton, you seem to be in the eye of this current storm."

Jaijo hesitated but stepped forward. "I am my father's son. My place is at his side." His hand joined theirs.

Gabriel grinned and threw his hand on top.

"I'm in it for the chance to make a profit. An' maybe a little for the adventure." He locked eyes with Matt. "But you've been a friend to me, Matt, an' I'll not see you stand alone against the likes of whatever Creighdor an' Scanlon an' their mates is."

Matt put his hand on top of theirs. The moment touched him. His father had never had anyone to truly trust like this.

Looking at his companions, Matt said, "Then let's be about it. Whatever Creighdor is doing, whatever he has planned, we're already behind him. We have to catch up." He took his hand away, adjusted the mummy head slung over his shoulder, and walked into the shadows of the buildings around him.

He knew the way wasn't going to be easy. But they had the mummy head, and they had the key that his father had left them.

It was a start on his private war against Lucius Creighdor. Once secrets began spilling out, they had a tendency to keep spilling. His father had told him that.

The trick was to stay alive.

ABOUT THE AUTHOR

Mel Odom is the author of many novels for adults, teens, and middle-grade readers. He lives with his family in Oklahoma. Visit him at www.melodom.net.